*"Why would son...
trouble of break...
without taking...*

Jason shook his head. "I don't know. Are you absolutely certain you locked that door?"

Emily shrugged. "I thought so. Now I'm not so sure."

Seeing the way she held herself, arms wrapped across her chest, he locked the door to her office and crossed to her side.

"What are you doing?"

Without a word, he gathered her close, pressing his mouth to a tangle of hair at her temple. Then he scooped her up and started into one of the examining rooms. He kicked the door shut and lowered his mouth to hers.

He murmured against her lips, "I've always found the best way to ponder a mystery is by doing something to divert attention."

"I see. Is that all I am? A diversion?"

He kissed her long and slow and deep, until heat rose up between them. "The best."

Available in March 2005 from Silhouette Sensation

Cover-Up
by Ruth Langan
(Devil's Cove)

Hidden Agenda
by Maggie Price
(Line of Duty)

Bring on the Night
by Sara Orwig
(Mission: Marriage)

Joint Forces
by Catherine Mann
(Wingmen Warriors)

Run to Me
by Lauren Nichols

Undercover Virgin
by Becky Barker

Cover-Up

RUTH LANGAN

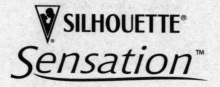

SILHOUETTE®

Sensation™

*First published in Great Britain 2005
Silhouette Books, Eton House, 18-24 Paradise Road,
Richmond, Surrey TW9 1SR*

© Ruth Ryan Langan 2004

ISBN 0 373 27355 X

18-0305

*Printed and bound in Spain
by Litografía Rosés S.A., Barcelona*

RUTH LANGAN

is an award-winning and bestselling author. Her books have been finalists for the Romance Writers of America's (RWA) RITA® Award. Married to her childhood sweetheart, she has raised five children and lives in Michigan, the state where she was born and raised. Ruth enjoys hearing from her readers. Letters can be sent via e-mail to ryanlangan@aol.com or via her website at www.ryanlangan.com

For my sisters,
Pat Brodzik and Margaret Griffith, with love.
And, of course, for Tom. Always.

Acknowledgements

I wish to thank Dr Scott Lewis and Melissa Lee of
Premier Internists for their valuable assistance.

Prologue

Devil's Cove, Michigan—1981

The boy plunged blindly through the woods, unmindful of the blackberry brambles that snagged his bloody T-shirt and ragged jeans. He barely noticed that it was raining, as the moss of the forest sucked at the soles of his sneakers, slowing his progress. He was desperate to reach his secret place. He'd come upon it by accident one day, when he'd been fleeing his father's drunken fury. A tiny cave, formed between two giant boulders. Just big enough for a small boy to hide and lick his wounds, safe from a world of violence.

There had been plenty of violence in Jason Cooper's young life. Whenever his father got liquored up, he came home itching for a fight. In the past he'd taken out his temper on his timid, frightened wife. But lately eight-year-old Jason had decided to become his mother's champion. Now his father got his kicks knocking his son around until he tired of the sport and passed out on the floor.

Jason's breath was coming in short bursts as he stumbled into his sanctuary and dropped to his knees.

At the realization that he wasn't alone his head came up sharply. "Who're you?"

The girl sat hunched against the far corner of the cave. Her white shorts and camp shirt were streaked with mud. Her knees, he noticed, were bloody. In her arms was a sleeping puppy.

"Emily. Emily Brennan. What's your name?"

"Jason Cooper." He glowered at her, annoyed at this intrusion. After all, this was his spot. His. He resented having to share it with anyone. "A tourist?"

The little town of Devil's Cove was littered with them during the summer. Visitors who flocked to the pretty beaches along the edge of Lake Michigan, ate in the fancy restaurants, shopped in the pricey gift shops. They clogged the highways and put money into the hands of local merchants. And, he thought bitterly, bought his father whiskey.

She shook her head, sending a honey-colored ponytail swinging. ''I live in town.''

''You're lost then?''

Again that shake of the head. ''I just wanted to get out of the rain.''

''What're you doing here in the woods?''

''I was trying to catch Buster.'' She looked adoringly at the puppy in her arms. ''Mr. Mulvahill called him the runt of the litter and said he was going to drown him. But Buster ran off before anyone could catch him. So I came after him.''

''That's pretty dumb. Why didn't you let him run away?''

''Dogs can't survive in the forest.''

''They can't survive drowning either. You bring him back, he's just going to be killed.''

She shivered and tightened her grasp on the bundle of fur. ''I'm taking him home as soon as the rain stops. My family will let me keep him.''

''Want to bet? Parents don't like strays. They'll probably just take him back to the Mulvahills.''

''No, they won't.'' She gave a vigorous shake of her head. ''Not when I tell them what Mr. Mulvahill plans to do. They've already let me keep two cats and a bunny. They won't say no to a little puppy.''

The small, caramel-colored pup woke up and yawned, then licked her face. With a smile she brushed a hand over its head, then looked at the boy. "Want to pet him?"

He scuttled closer and touched a hand to the downy softness. And felt the first ragged edge of anger begin to slip away. "He's ugly."

"No, he isn't. He's just dirty. I'll clean him and he'll look just fine. You'll see." After a few minutes Emily reached into the pocket of her shorts and unwrapped a package of cheese crackers. "Want some?"

He helped himself to a couple and the two of them chewed in contented silence.

She glanced at the blood staining his shirt. "You're all wet. And you've cut yourself."

"Doesn't matter." Up close he found himself looking into wide honey eyes. Trusting eyes, he thought. As trusting as the puppy's. "What'd you do to your knees?"

She glanced down and shrugged. "Fell over a log."

"Won't your folks be mad about all that mud?"

"Uh-uh." Again that toss of the head, sending

her ponytail swinging. "Poppie says I'm always coming home looking like I fought with a bear."

"Who's Poppie?"

"My grandfather. But Bert says whoever I fight with, I'll always win."

"Who's Bert?"

"My grandma."

"You call your grandmother Bert?"

"Everybody does. We live with my grandparents."

"Why?"

She shrugged. "I don't know. We just always have." She offered him more crackers, and when he refused, she placed three in his hand before popping the last three into her mouth.

Maybe it was her sense of fairness. Or maybe it was simply the calm way in which she accepted him. Whatever the reason, Jason felt more anger begin to dissipate in her company. "We moved here a month ago."

"I'm glad." She gave him a wide smile that put sunshine to shame. "We can be friends."

Before he could answer she glanced at the entrance of the cave. "Rain's stopped." She got to her feet. "I'd better get Buster home. Want to come?"

It was on the tip of his tongue to refuse. But he found he didn't want to be alone just yet. Odd, since he'd always preferred his own company to that of others. "Sure. How far's home?"

"Not far." She led the way outside and held the pup close to her chest as she tramped through the woods.

When they reached the edge of town, Jason expected Emily to lead him toward the converted cottages and trailer parks that dotted the working-class section of town. Instead she turned to the mansions that sat in a row along the water's edge.

She started up the driveway of a sprawling white house with a sign that read The Willows.

Jason held back. "You live here?"

She nodded. "Come on."

Though he had his doubts that he'd be welcome, he couldn't resist the urge to see how such people lived.

"Hi, Em. What have you got there?" A red-haired, freckled imp looked up from a glass-topped patio table where she sat drawing.

"A puppy. This is Jason. That's my sister, Sidney."

"Hi, Jason." The imp grinned and returned her attention to her watercolors.

"Sidney." He was still staring at her and nearly tripped over another imp, this one carrying a hose and with wet blond bangs dripping into her eyes.

"Out of my way," she shouted. "Poppie needs my help in the garden."

As she raced past them Emily called, "Hannah, say hi to Jason."

"Hi." A chubby fist was raised before she disappeared around the corner of the house.

"You got any more sisters?"

"Just Courtney. She's probably down at the water's edge. That's all of us. And my mom and dad and Bert and Poppie."

His stomach clenched at the thought of so many people. But to his amazement, he was accepted without question when he walked inside. After quick introductions to her grandmother and the housekeeper, he and Emily were sent off to locate a box and blanket for the puppy.

Minutes later, while they chose a cozy spot in the kitchen for Buster, Emily's grandmother asked the housekeeper, Trudy, to make them lemonade.

After polishing off two tall glasses, Bert gestured toward the laundry room. "Time to wash off that mud, you two."

She stood watching as they scrubbed, then handed them fluffy yellow towels. When she spotted the blood on Jason's shirt, the old woman held out a hand. "Give me that and I'll have Trudy wash it before you go home."

He gave a quick shake of his head. "No need. My ma'll see to it."

"You may need a little disinfectant. That's a lot of blood."

The lie came easily. "I fell off my bike."

"All the more reason to take a look at that cut." Before he could argue the housekeeper was there beside them, tugging off his shirt.

"Mother of God…"

He was too young to know about the scars that crisscrossed his back. But he was aware of the sudden silence and glanced up in time to see the look Trudy exchanged with Emily's grandmother before applying ointment ever so gently.

Bert insisted on feeding him. An egg salad sandwich. A frosty glass of milk. A banana. And when he was leaving, she asked the housekeeper to send along a handful of chocolate chip cookies for his walk home.

For an eight-year-old boy who had never known tenderness, this day had been like a soothing balm. One he would never forget. And though he was intrigued by the kindness of the old woman in the wonderful white mansion, it was her granddaughter with the bloody knees, the smile of an angel and a fondness for strays who had completely captured his heart.

Chapter 1

The fog rolled in, blanketing the entire shore, forcing the boats that were caught in it to use their sonar devices to avoid the treacherous rocks that lay in wait for them. That deadly combination of fog and rocks had been the reason seventeenth-century sailors had given this area the name Devil's Cove. The skeletons of shipwrecks that lay on the lake's floor were a reminder of deadlier times, and had become a haven for divers searching for treasures. The town had seen its share of pirates, paupers, playboys and charlatans. And though Devil's Cove was now a prosperous resort town, with restored mansions and upscale shopping and dining, there remained about it an aura of mystery and intrigue.

As morning sunlight burned off the last wisps of fog, the town seemed to spring to life, ready for another day of surprises for those who called it home.

Jason Cooper turned the rental car off the highway at the top of the hill and switched off the ignition before stepping out. Below him, the houses, streets and parks of Devil's Cove were clearly visible. There was Devil's Cove High School sporting a new track and football field. The Methodist church on the corner of Park and Main looked as regal as ever. A memorial for sailors lost in the Great Lakes sat in the park in the center of town. The grass was neatly trimmed and decorated with American flags and red, white and blue flowers in pretty pots.

He breathed in the familiar scents of water and earth and forest and realized his heart was pounding. Home. And yet not home. This hadn't been home for him in more than ten years. When he'd lived here, all he'd thought about was running away. It didn't matter where he went, as long as he got as far away from Devil's Cove as possible.

And yet here he was, back where it had all started.

Though much of it looked the same, it was plain that there had been tremendous growth in this area since he'd been gone. The steady hum of construction equipment could be heard in the distance, and he could see that much of the pristine forest had been carved into roads leading to housing developments.

He'd often wondered how long it would take for people to discover the beauty of this northern Michigan playground. The lure of clear lakes and pine forests made the land far too valuable to remain farmland forever.

He climbed back into the car and headed toward town. Up ahead he saw the Harbor House. As he drove along the curving ribbon of driveway and waited for someone to take his bags, he steeled himself against the wave of feelings that nearly overwhelmed him.

He was here, he reminded himself, because he chose to be. If he changed his mind tomorrow and decided to get the hell out, there was nobody who could stop him.

As the valet took his car keys he strode inside the Harbor House and registered for his room. Without bothering to unpack, he made his way to the dining room. What he needed was good food and hot coffee. Then he'd see the town at his leisure.

"Well, well." Hannah Brennan, in ragged jeans and T-shirt, looked up from the salad she was tossing to grin at her sister, Emily. "I see you always manage to get rid of your patients just in time for lunch, Doctor. Do you just leave them waiting in the sick room?"

"Too easy. I drug them and leave them locked in the examining room. They'll never even miss me." Emily plucked a tomato wedge from the bowl and popped it in her mouth. "I see by the conditions of those jeans that you've been digging in the dirt again, baby sis."

"Comes with the territory. I'm finishing up Dr. Applegate's flower beds. Lucky for you, I scrubbed my fingernails before tackling this salad."

"Thank heaven for small favors."

"You're welcome. I know what a fanatic you doctors can be about clean hands."

Emily paused a moment to study the scene of controlled chaos on the patio. Her grandfather muttering as he wrestled with a foot-long salmon he was about to grill. Her grandmother untangling the fasteners on the patio umbrella. Her mother parceling out chores like a general, while her sisters made themselves useful. And underfoot an array of pets left over from Emily's childhood passion for strays. An ancient gray-and-white tabby with a missing ear dozing in a pool of sunlight. A brown mutt with oversize paws that Emily had rescued from a Dumpster during her internship at University Hospital. A pair of white rabbits that had been found on the Brennan porch a few weeks after Easter, presumably left there by parents who had made a hasty purchase and knew which bleeding hearts would be willing to give them shelter.

It was a scene Emily had been enjoying since she was born. The Brennan family had lived in this big house for three generations. Their home, The Willows, was part of a wonderful collection of turn-of-the-century mansions that sat along the shore of Lake Michigan, hugging the water's edge like faded dowagers.

Emily's grandparents had bought the house more than fifty years ago, and had immersed themselves in the life of the community. Her grandfather, Frank Brennan, was a retired judge and gentleman farmer, though his gardens now contained flowers instead of vegetables. He spent every spare moment working on his inventions, though no one could recall one that served any particular purpose other than to amuse him.

His wife, Alberta, an English teacher whom the family affectionately called Bert, had been a fixture at the local high school for four decades. Her announcement that she was retiring had left the community, and her family, stunned.

Bert was a sea of calm in this stormy, volatile family of achievers. Emily glanced at her with affection. If the world were coming to an end, her grandmother would find something soothing to say about it.

When her son Christopher had returned from a medical internship in Chicago with his bride Charlotte, called Charley by all who knew her, a wing had been added to The Willows for the newlyweds. Chris and his beautiful Charley had quickly been absorbed into the house, and into the community as well. Chris established himself as town doctor, and had built a clinic in the rear of the house. Charley raised their four daughters while starting her own real estate firm, which now routinely handled the sale of million-dollar houses being built on the few remaining parcels of waterfront land.

"I'm glad you could get away to join us for lunch, Em." Charley was wrapping vegetables in foil, crimping the edges to hold the moisture before placing them on the grill.

"I wouldn't miss it. Especially today." Emily crossed the brick-paved patio furnished with a mix of contemporary wrought-iron furniture and comfortable heirloom wicker pieces that her sister Courtney had found for her grandparents on her last buying trip to Europe. Courtney owned a gift shop in town, and lived in the tiny apartment above it. Her impeccable taste was reflected in the pots of geraniums and ivy offering bright islands of color on the terraced lawn that sloped to the water's edge.

Emily smiled at the sight of her sister Sidney arranging pale-pink roses and baby's breath in a vase. To an artist like Sid, the color, the symmetry, the beauty of the presentation, were as essential as the food they would eat. In fact, it wouldn't surprise Emily to learn that her sister simply forgot to eat for days at a time. How else did she explain that tiny figure?

"It's a grand day, isn't it?" Bert continued setting the table with colorful napkins and pretty crystal plates.

All that was missing to complete this cozy picture, Emily thought with a quick flash of pain, was her father. When she'd left Devil's Cove to pursue a medical career at University Hospital, he'd been so proud that one of his children was following in his footsteps. It had never occurred to her that he wouldn't be around for years to offer sage advice.

Emily had thought her days in her grandparents' house, like those of her three sisters, would consist mainly of occasional visits. Yet here she was keeping a deathbed promise to her father to carry on his practice until a replacement could be found, and living once again in her childhood home.

It hadn't been easy giving up her hard-won independence. Still, her family seemed to understand, and worked hard at giving her the space she needed to make the adjustment.

Her grandfather looked up from the grill. "Emily, we could use those fine surgeon's hands to fillet this salmon."

That brought a round of laughter from the others.

Though Frank Brennan had traded in his judicial robes for a golf shirt and casual slacks more than a dozen years ago, he still had a commanding courtroom presence, which he used to his advantage whenever it suited him.

Emily joined in the laughter. "I always knew my medical training would come in handy for something, Poppie.'' Her childhood nickname for him rolled easily off her tongue.

''That's my girl.'' He brushed a kiss over Emily's cheek as she picked up a knife and neatly sliced through the fish.

He arranged the fillets on the grill and was rewarded by the hiss and snap of the fire as they began to cook.

''Trudy,'' he bellowed, and turned to find their housekeeper standing right behind him. ''Why do you always sneak up on me like that?''

''I don't sneak.'' Trudy Carpenter was as wide as she was tall, with big capable hands and a voice, after a lifetime of smoking three packs a day, that sounded like a rusty hinge. Her face was deeply lined, her hair the color and texture of cotton balls.

His tone was accusing. ''You blindsided me.''

''Easy enough to do, since you never look before hollering.'' The old woman sniffed and held out a tray of glasses. ''Judge, Miss Bert says you're to drink a tall glass of water before lunch.''

''Let Bert drink the water.'' He picked up a tumbler of his favorite Scotch and winked at his granddaughter before lifting it to his lips.

''Beats me why you always try to fight it.'' Emily gave him a quick nudge with her elbow. This was an argument these old people had been waging for a lifetime. One they seemed to thoroughly enjoy. "You'll just have to drink the water later."

"Later is better than now." He grinned. "I'll have food in my stomach later."

Overhearing him, Hannah gave a throaty laugh. "You'd better hope you never have to give Poppie any medicine, Em. If you think he's finicky about water, wait till you see him try to swallow something nasty."

Emily grinned. "I'll make sure it's cherry-flavored, like the medicine we give the children."

"That'll work," his wife called from across the patio. "Since he's just a big kid at heart."

"And you like me that way, Bert." He blew her a kiss before turning the salmon, all the while muttering that he needed to invent a better spatula.

His family had no doubt that would be his next project.

When the fish was ready, he transferred it to a platter and the family took their places around the glass-topped table. Frank Brennan was in his favorite wicker chair, sporting the contented look he always wore when surrounded by his women. His handsome Irish face was deeply creased with laugh lines. His lion's mane of white hair showed off his ruddy complexion, made even deeper by the summer sun.

His wife was seated at the other end of the table, her soft cap of gray curls dancing in the breeze that perpetually blew off the waters of Lake Michigan.

Charley sat on one side of the table, between Hannah and Courtney, while Emily and Sidney sat across from them.

Emily passed a basket of rolls to her grandmother. "I still can't believe your retirement party is this week. Are you ready for your big kickoff night?"

"Probably more so than you. I hear the tribute committee has been pestering you with calls all morning."

Emily sighed. "Now I know why they asked me to be the chairman of this tribute. Every time they need something done, they call their chairman and dump it all in my lap."

Hannah looked around the table and grinned. "That's because you have Sucker written on your forehead."

Emily joined in the laughter at her expense and accepted a piece of salmon, then held the platter while her grandmother selected one for herself. "I didn't have a clue what I was signing up for."

"It'll soon be over and you can get back to a normal life." Frank took a taste of salmon. Pleased with his efforts, he tucked into his meal.

"I have a bit of news." Charley paused to glance at her family. "You know the developer that bought that last big chunk of Prentice Osborn's lakeside property?"

The others nodded.

"The rumors were all true. The town council approved his plan to build homes and condominiums around a world-class golf course, yacht club, restaurants and shops." She paused a beat before saying softly, "My agency will be representing it."

"Oh, Mom." Hannah gave her mother a fierce hug, before Courtney pressed a kiss to her mother's cheek.

Sidney and Emily were on their feet and racing around the table to do the same.

"Christopher would be so proud of you, Charley." Frank lifted his glass in a salute and the others joined him.

Charley glanced at her daughters. "Actually this development has been a boon for all the Brennans. The architect's interior designer has already given Courtney a list of some of the things he'll be wanting for the models. And when he saw some of Sidney's work, he decided to commission her to paint a mural on the walls of the foyer. There's talk of having her do the ceiling of the dining room as well.''

At the news, Sidney beamed. ''Mom, are you sure?''

Charley grinned at the sweet redhead who had always been the dreamy artist in the family. Since losing her young fiancé to illness two years earlier, she'd become even more introverted and reclusive. Though her family was concerned, they knew she had to work through the grief in her own time.

''I'm sure. And I'm sure whatever you paint will be the talk of the town.'' She sipped her lemonade before adding, ''On top of that, Hannah has been given the contract for all the landscaping.''

Her grandfather arched a brow at his grand-daughter. ''That ought to pay your greenhouse loan for a year or two.''

That had them all smiling. Hannah had gone deeply into debt to finance new greenhouses for her fledgling nursery and landscape business.

She ran her fingers through her short blond bob. ''This is a dream job. When Mom told me, I didn't believe her at first. But now that I've had a chance to look at the blueprints, I realize I'll have to double or even triple my crew to handle it. Not that I'm complaining. By the time I'm through with this contract, there won't be anyone in Devil's Cove who hasn't heard of Hannah's Gardening and Landscape.''

Her grandfather looked at her with affection. ''I always knew your knack for gardening would pay off one day. You inherited that from me.''

''Speaking of inheritance...'' Emily took a final bite of salmon before pushing away from the table. ''I have to get back to the clinic. I want to leave early this afternoon so I can see what the committee did with the decorations for tonight's kickoff cocktail party.'' She paused by her grandmother's side and bent to press a kiss to her cheek before rounding the table to do the same to her mother. ''I'm so proud of you, Mom.''

''Thanks, honey.''

''But I think you're about to become awfully busy.''

''I don't mind. I can't wait.'' Charlotte laid a hand on her daughter's arm. ''We'll all see you at the party tonight. I know you and your committee will do a fine job.''

After kissing her grandfather and congratulating her sisters on their good news, Emily made her way inside. A glance at the clock told her she had less than five minutes before her first afternoon patient. She hurried toward the clinic at the rear of the house.

Chapter 2

"You just about finished, Doc?" The sixteen-year-old boy lying on the examining table had his teeth clenched so tightly he could hardly get the question out.

"Almost done, Cody." Emily tied off the final stitch while her assistant, Melissa, mopped at the blood on the boy's thigh. "Just another minute."

When she finished, Emily straightened, slipping off her latex gloves, and turned to the boy's mother, who was hovering in a far corner of the examining room, looking anywhere but at her son's bloody calf. "Janet, I'll give you a prescription for pain so Cody can sleep tonight."

"I don't need stuff for pain." The boy swung his legs over the side of the table and turned pasty-white as the blood rushed from his head. He looked down at the crimson stains that smeared the front of his baseball uniform and swallowed hard.

"You may not think so now," Emily steadied him with a hand to his shoulder, giving him a chance to clear his head without embarrassing him. "But when this wears off you might want to have something, just in case."

When his color returned she crossed the room and wrote on a notepad, then tore off the page and handed it to his mother. "He'll be fine, Janet. But he ought to skip practice until those stitches come out. I wouldn't want to see him tear that wound open."

"Thanks, Dr. Brennan." Janet Adams gave a laugh as she shook her head from side to side. "Dr. Brennan. Seems like I've been saying that all my life. Except now it's to you instead of your father." She looked down at the prescription, avoiding Emily's eyes. "I'm glad you've stayed on in Devil's Cove. The town just wouldn't feel the same without a Doctor Brennan in it."

"That's nice." Emily felt a twinge of pain before she managed a smile. "Next time you dive for home plate, Cody, try to avoid the other guy's spikes.''

''Okay, Doc.'' The boy grinned self-consciously.

As he eased off the table and headed toward the door Emily stopped him. ''By the way, Cody. Who won?''

''We did, Doc. By one run.''

She laughed. ''I guess that's worth a few stitches.''

''You bet.''

She was still laughing when the boy and his mother left.

She turned to her assistant. ''Is that the last patient?''

Melissa shook her head. ''Prentice Osborn is here with his brother, Will. I put them in the other room.''

The Osborn family was the most prominent in Devil's Cove. Prentice, a former classmate of Emily's, had more than doubled his family fortune in the past ten years. It was his grandfather who'd had the foresight to buy up the choice acreage dotted with farms. In recent years a bidding war by developers eager to build hotels and condos on the property had made Prentice more money than his grandfather could have ever dreamed possible.

Even if Prentice hadn't turned a fortune, the townspeople would have admired him for his tireless care of his severely handicapped brother. Will Osborn, with his garbled speech and unsteady gait, was treated gently by all the citizens of Devil's Cove. He was routinely handed his favorite sugar cookies at the bakery. Whenever he visited the diner he was given a grilled cheese sandwich and a chocolate malt, free of charge.

To thank them, Prentice was more than generous to the town that sheltered his brother. He gave freely of his time and money to various charities around town. A new wing at the University Hospital now bore the names of his deceased parents.

Emily smiled at the two men. "Hello, Prentice. Will. What brings you here?"

Prentice Osborn, tall, with sun-streaked golden hair, took charge. "Will's been tugging on his ear. I think it's another infection."

Emily turned to the older brother, who was watching her with the wary eyes of a frightened child, so at odds with his almost graying hair and stooped shoulders. "Have you been swimming in the mill pond again, Will?"

The man shrugged and stared hard at the floor.

"It's okay, Will." Prentice spoke to his brother the way one would speak to a child. "You can tell

Dr. Brennan the truth. Have you been swimming in the mill pond?''

His brother nodded shyly.

''Well, let's have a look.''

Before Emily could step closer Will hunched his shoulders and cringed.

Prentice sent her a pleading look. ''Will was poked and prodded by too many doctors when he was young. Do you think you could give him a sedative to take the edge off his nerves?''

Emily nodded her understanding and reached for a syringe. ''This won't hurt, Will.'' She moved so quickly he didn't even have time to react. To his brother she said, ''Dilaudid. Just two milligrams. Enough to quiet him, but not so much he'll have any reaction. Now, Will.'' She indicated the examining table and the shy man sat on the edge and watched as she sorted through her instruments. When she bent close he breathed her in and, relaxed now and enjoying the faint scent of her perfume, grinned like an errant schoolboy.

It took only a moment's examination to see the evidence. ''I'll bet this has been giving you some pain, Will.''

He nodded.

''It'll be much improved by tomorrow.'' She used a dropper to dispense liquid into the ear, then wrote on a notepad and tore it off, handing it to his brother. "He'll need to take this antibiotic for a full ten days. I'll want to see him then, to make certain the infection is completely cleared up."

Prentice put an arm around his brother's shoulders. "Come on, Will. Let's go home and take Dr. Brennan's medicine. Before you know it you'll be feeling as good as new." He helped his brother from the table. As he followed Will from the room he turned. "Would you like me to pick you up for tonight's cocktail party, Emily?"

She shook her head. "Thanks, Prentice. But I'll be heading up there early to see to some of the last-minute details."

"Then I'll see you there."

When he and Will were gone, Emily looked up as Melissa poked her head in the examining room. "You've had three calls in the last hour from the tribute committee. They're waiting for you at the Harbor House. They want you to check out the ballroom for tonight's kickoff party."

Emily sighed. "Why did I ever agree to chair this tribute to my grandmother?"

"Because you love her. We all do. And because nobody else in town was willing to see to all the little details the way you do."

"Yeah." Emily laughed. "Like they say, the

devil is in the details.'' She began unbuttoning her white lab coat. ''I'll run over to the Harbor House and see what they've done. But I have no intention of getting roped into making any changes in the decorations at this late date.''

''Right.'' Melissa nodded her head. ''And I believe that as much as I believe Cody Fletcher is going to skip baseball practice until his stitches come out.''

''Am I that transparent?'' Emily sighed. ''Don't answer that, Mel.'' She unlocked the door that separated the clinic from the main house. ''I'll see you in the morning.''

She pulled the door shut before making her way up the back staircase to the second floor. In her old bedroom she stopped to scratch behind the ears of a white kitten stretched out on her bed.

''You're shedding, Angel. That's why you've been banished from the clinic. Mel said she's sick and tired of sweeping up after you. Besides, there are actually a few patients who are allergic to all that dander.''

The cat yawned and licked a paw with a bored expression.

Grinning, Emily stripped off the simple skirt and blouse she'd worn under her lab coat and slipped into a pair of faded jeans and a T-shirt. It was best to be prepared, she thought with a quick glance in the mirror, in case the committee needed her help with last-minute decorations. She might talk a good game to Melissa, but she knew she'd end up pitching in with the work.

"I'll leave the door open," she called to the cat. "Maybe you'll take the hint and shed somewhere else."

Once in the car Emily opened the window and let the breeze take the ends of her hair as she mulled the path her life had taken. It was hard to believe she'd been back in Devil's Cove for six months now, first to take care of her father, and then to take over his practice. The days and weeks had a way of blurring together here. At University Hospital there had been staff meetings, luncheons, daily tours of patients' rooms and in-depth discussions of various treatments. Not to mention late-night dinners with David where, more often than not, they ended up debating articles they'd read in medical journals, or the latest controversial drugs being tested by a colleague.

David was Dr. David Turnley, a specialist in pediatric surgery who had hoped to persuade Emily to be his partner, not only in his professional life but in his personal life as well. It caught her by surprise to admit that there'd been no time to miss him since she'd returned home.

Here the care was much more personal in nature. She wasn't just part of a team. She was a hands-on small-town doctor who was expected to stitch wounds, deliver babies, treat infections and dispense advice on everything from obesity to high blood pressure to clinical depression.

It felt good, she realized as she eased her car to the curb. For however long she stayed, it felt good to be back.

She turned off the ignition and studied the sprawling old inn that had graced the town of Devil's Cove for more than eighty years. Painted white, with a gleaming black roof and black shutters, it was both stylish and graceful. A wide pillared porch along the front was dotted with white wicker furniture and pots of colorful flowers and trailing ivy. On one side was a lovely formal garden that sported curving stone walkways leading to a gazebo in the middle, which was often used for wedding receptions.

Emily made her way up the steps and inside the foyer, where Beth Collins, a college student home for the summer, was busy taking a phone reservation. She waved as Emily passed, then returned her attention to the guest register.

When Emily reached the ballroom she could hear the squeals of laughter even before she opened the double doors. She stepped inside to see half a dozen women huddled together while one harried-looking woman in bright pink sneakers stood in the middle of the room holding tightly to at least a hundred streamers attached to balloons.

"If someone doesn't help me soon," Marge Dawson pleaded, "I swear I'll float all the way to the ceiling."

"So will I," another woman shouted. "And I won't even need a balloon."

There was a louder burst of giggles from the cluster of women.

"Okay, what's going on?" Emily glanced around. "It looks like our tribute committee has been dipping into the punch."

"Emily." One woman separated herself from the others and rushed forward. "Wait 'til you hear." She paused, her hand on her heart. "You'll never guess who checked into the Harbor House today."

"From the looks of all of you, Libby, I'd have to say Brad Pitt."

"Even better." Libby Conway tucked a strand of red hair behind her ear. Her freckles seemed even more pronounced than ever now that her face was flushed.

The others nodded and gathered around, ignoring the pleadings of their friend with the balloons.

"Jason Cooper." The name was spoken on a sigh. "Can you believe Jason Cooper is here in Devil's Cove?"

Emily's smile faded just a notch.

Seeing it, one of the women asked, "Didn't you know he was coming, Emily? I mean, you *are* chairing this event."

Emily didn't quite trust her voice, so she merely shook her head.

"Did he even acknowledge the invitation?" another asked.

"No." Emily was glad to note that her voice sounded as steady as ever. She hoped whatever turmoil was going on inside wasn't visible to these women.

"Well, how can you expect someone as famous as Jason Cooper to answer every invitation he gets?" Libby giggled. " Have you read his latest book?"

"Hasn't the whole world?" one of the women remarked.

There was a rush of nervous laughter.

"It was creepy," one of them said. "The town

in his book resembled Devil's Cove. All those gory murders. I couldn't put it down.''

''Me either.'' A slender brunette shivered, then added, ''I wonder why he didn't tell anyone he was coming.''

''Too busy. He probably has a secretary to handle such things.''

At Libby's words, the others nodded their agreement.

''Yeah. And an agent, and a public relations firm and a business manager and...''

''And dozens of gorgeous models and actresses falling all over him.''

''Can you blame them?'' A perky blonde lowered her voice to a whisper. ''Did you see that article about him in *Celebrity?*''

A woman whose dark hair was streaked with gray nodded. ''You mean the one showing him on the deck of that mansion he bought in Malibu? They said he never grants interviews. He jogs before the sun comes up. He works all night, sleeps all day, and keeps his private life extremely private. He looked like the dark, brooding hero of every one of his books. I thought I'd die.''

The others sighed their agreement.

''Guess where he went as soon as he checked in?'' Libby lowered her voice, even though everyone in the room knew the answer to that except Emily.

Emily shrugged. ''I can't imagine.''

''To the Daisy Diner. You know who works there, don't you?''

Emily didn't need to respond. In a town as small as Devil's Cove, everyone knew where everyone worked. And it was no secret that Carrie Lester, an old classmate, had been working there for years.

Emily kept her tone steady. ''That's really nice. Jason and Carrie's brother, Cory, were best friends.''

Libby gave a short laugh. ''Maybe Cory wasn't his only best friend. You know…'' She looked around at the others for confirmation. ''…I've always thought Carrie's little girl had eyes like a certain bestselling author and playboy who was once known as the bad boy of Devil's Cove.''

''I think we'd better get those balloons up and head home.'' Emily's throat felt so tight, she could hardly get the words out.

''Okay.'' Libby shrugged. ''Emily's right. We'd better move it if we want to look glamorous for the cocktail party tonight. And now that we've got Jason Cooper in our midst, we have to look our best. Connie, help Marge get those balloons in place.''

When the others walked away, Emily let out a long, slow breath.

Jason Cooper. Here in Devil's Cove.

She hadn't seen him since she was eighteen. He'd left town the day after graduation, without a word to anyone. Like Libby, there were many who thought it was because Carrie Lester was carrying his baby. Emily had never believed that. Not then. Not now. Still, it hurt to know that in all the time they'd been apart, he'd never made a single attempt to contact her. And now, after all this time, it was Carrie he went to see.

She shrugged it off. She'd worked hard to put Jason Cooper out of her mind. And she'd succeeded. Now he was nothing more than a bittersweet memory of earlier, innocent times.

"What about that banner?" Emily started toward the stage. There was no way she was going to stand idly by and pick at old wounds. "Can somebody give me a hand putting this up?"

She caught hold of a ladder and began to climb. This was what she needed. Nothing like good hard physical work to keep the mind from going into overdrive.

"Jason." Carrie Lester sloshed coffee over the rim of the cup she was carrying. She hissed a

breath and folded a paper napkin in the saucer before handing it to Teddy Morton, one of her regulars. Then she rounded the counter and paused to
study the darkly handsome man who stood framed
in the doorway. "You look..." She shook her
head. "...different...successful."

"Is that the best you can do?" He arched a brow
before striding toward the sister of his best friend
and kissing her cheek. "You look as pretty as
ever."

"Yeah. Right." She touched a hand to her
cheek. "Men get better as they get older. Women
just get older."

He tugged on a lock of hair the color of plati-
•num. "What're you now? Twenty-seven? Twenty-
eight? How can you call that old?"

"I've got a ten-year-old kid. There are days
when that makes me feel really ancient." She indicated an empty booth. "You want to sit and I'll
get you some coffee?"

"I'd rather sit at the counter. That way you can
talk to me while you work." He settled himself on
a stool and waited while she poured him a cup of
black coffee.

"What time did you get in, Jason?"

"An hour ago." He sipped. Paused.

Carrie leaned her elbows on the counter and

lowered her voice, knowing the regulars were
watching and listening. After all, it wasn't every
day the Daisy Diner entertained a celebrity. "I
couldn't believe it when Mrs. B. announced that
she was retiring." She gave a self-conscious laugh.
"I know you're not going to believe this, after all
the trouble I gave her when we were in school, but
I was hoping she'd be around to teach Jenny."

"Yeah. I know what you mean. She was the
toughest old bird I've ever met. But she was the
only adult in this town who ever cared about me."

"Yeah. She really liked you, Jason."

He managed a smile. "By the way, how's your
mom, Carrie?"

"Fine. Still working for the Osborns. She gives
me a hand with Jenny on the weekends if I have
to pull a double shift." She walked away to wait
on a customer. Minutes later she returned to con-
tinue the conversation as though there had been no
interruption. "She keeps talking about retiring, but
she just can't do it yet." She picked up the cof-
feepot and topped off his cup, then moved along
the counter, filling others.

After ringing up several payments she returned.
"You want something to eat?"

He shook his head. "I ate at the Harbor House.
They make the best grilled salmon in the world."

Carrie grinned. "You ought to try my grilled cheese. With bread-and-butter pickles. And for dessert, a hot fudge sundae with a sprinkling of peanuts."

He grinned. "Nothing ever changes around Devil's Cove."

Carrie's look grew thoughtful. She leaned closer. "I wish I'd had the courage to leave like you did, Jason."

"You still can, Carrie."

"No, I can't. It's too late for me."

"It's never too late."

She huffed out a breath. "Now you sound like Mrs. B."

"Do I?" He frowned. "I don't know why that should surprise me. She colored every decision I've ever made. Even years after I left here, I could hear her voice in my head."

"Is that why you came for the tribute?"

Before he could answer she excused herself to wait on another customer. Jason sat staring into his coffee and thinking about the question. He'd told himself a hundred times that he was coming here because of his old teacher who had made such a difference in his life. He owed it to her to be here. Hell, he owed her everything. She'd been his refuge from a nightmare life with a father who was a drunk and a bully, and a mother who was terrified to leave him. To spare his mother, Jason had often taken the beatings meant for her. And he had the scars to prove it.

His old teacher had been able to see through the wall of anger he'd built around himself. Anger that masked a bright mind and an iron will. Despite his bad-boy image, Mrs. Brennan had loaned him books, got him summer jobs and encouraged him when no one else did. When the opportunity to escape had been dropped into his lap, he'd gone to her for advice. She'd given it in a few terse words. "Take the gift you're being offered. And hone your skills, boy."

Hone your skills.

It had taken him a while to figure out what they were. He'd mended fences on a ranch in Texas, manicured fairways on a golf course in Arizona, bussed tables in L.A. And all the while he'd observed, and written copious notes in a journal. His first novel had been hailed as brilliant, his second riveting and his third had lifted him into the rarified stratosphere of superstar. His current book was considered by critics to be his best yet. Still, it was bound to make him a pariah in his hometown. He'd opened up old wounds by chronicling a string of murders that had happened right here.

He'd welcomed this opportunity to come back to Devil's Cove and publicly thank the woman who had opened his mind to the possibilities. She'd been a refuge for a confused, angry boy. Without Mrs. B., there was no telling what choices he might have made. But there was another reason he was here. When he'd read the letter detailing the tribute planned for his old teacher, it was the name of the person chairing the committee that had leapt off the page.

Emily Brennan.

Emily was back in town. It might be his last chance, his only chance, to see her and try to make things right between them.

He had no idea how she would react. Or how he'd feel when he saw her again. He had, after all, left her without a word. And in the ten years since then, they'd had no contact.

A part of him hoped she had changed. Had become polished, sleek, sophisticated, maybe a little brittle, a little hard around the edges. It would be easier that way. He could go back to the life he'd made for himself without regrets. But in a small part of his mind he couldn't help hoping that her sweetness, her kindness, her wonderful, simple optimism had remained. It had always been what had set Emily Brennan apart. Despite her family's

wealth and standing in the community, she'd
seemed completely unaffected by it. There was a
tenderheartedness about her, a way of accepting
strays, both animal and human, that had always
been so endearing to a boy whose life had been
devoid of tenderness.

He had, quite simply, loved her. From the first
time he'd seen her, seeking refuge in his hideaway,
ignoring the scrapes on her knees to rescue a
puppy, he'd fallen with a thud. By the time he'd
left Devil's Cove, he'd begun to believe that she
loved him as well. But he'd learned that hearts,
like people, change. He might be clever at min-
gling fact with fiction, but he was smart enough to
know that it was impossible to revive something
that was long dead.

And so he'd come back to Devil's Cove to honor
an old teacher and see an old love one last time.
Then, he hoped, he could turn his back on the town
of his childhood forever. This time, with no regrets.

Chapter 3

Emily fastened small diamond studs in her ears before stepping back to study her reflection in the mirror. Her dress was a long smooth column of emerald silk with a square neckline, long sleeves and a sweeping hemline that ended just above her ankles. It wasn't the one she'd intended to wear tonight, but she'd decided at the last minute that the black silk with the lace jacket was too ordinary. After fussing with the decorations long after the rest of her committee had gone home, she'd realized that the last thing she wanted tonight was to appear ordinary. Since dazzling wasn't her style, she had to settle for elegant.

Let Jason Cooper ignore her in this.

The thought had her going very still. Was that what this was about? Trying to get Jason to notice her?

She studied herself more carefully, then slowly shook her head. Not notice. Regret. She wanted him to regret having left her behind. Without a word. That's what hurt the most.

She'd always known Jason would leave. Hadn't they talked about it a hundred times? He'd always said he would leave as soon as he graduated and never look back. But always, when they'd talked of it, he'd promised to take her along. It wasn't just his dream; it was theirs. And he'd robbed her of it.

Not robbed, exactly, she admitted. After all, her privileged lifestyle had allowed her to come and go at will, first attending the University of Michigan and later studying medicine at Georgetown. But until Jason's first book had been published, amid a storm of publicity, she hadn't known where he was, or even if he was alive or dead. That's what had hurt the most. While she'd been worrying herself half sick, fearing the worst, he'd been traveling the country, having a grand old time, finding himself, writing books. But never writing to her. Not a letter. Not a postcard.

Some writer, she thought.

She picked up the small emerald beaded hand-bag and started down the stairs. With a wry smile she whispered, "I hope you eat your heart out, Jason Cooper."

It was a perfect summer evening. The warm breeze off Lake Michigan was perfumed with the fragrance of roses that graced the gardens of Harbor House. Throngs of people lined the porch of the inn and spilled down the steps onto the side-walk. The top of the porch had been strung with festive lanterns that winked and swayed.

Inside, people were lined up in front of a long table to present their tickets and collect their name tags before entering the ballroom. Emily was pleased to note that the welcome committee had added extra members to handle the crowd.

Libby Conway spotted her and hurried over, looking her up and down as she did. "Wow. You didn't buy that in Devil's Cove."

Emily laughed. "New York. Last year when I was there for a medical convention."

Libby lowered her voice. "You're not going to believe this. Guess who showed up tonight?"

Emily shrugged.

"Robeson Ryder."

"Robeson?" Emily's eyes lit with pleasure at the mention of the fiery civil rights leader who now made his home in Chicago. "Oh, that's wonderful. He'd sent word earlier that he didn't know if he'd be able to make it. My grandmother will be so happy."

"Not to mention a few hundred people here to-night who see him as their savior." Libby glanced around as the crowd continued to grow. "It's strange having so many unfamiliar faces in town. Where did they all come from?"

Emily squeezed her hand. "Isn't it a wonderful tribute to my grandmother that so many of her for-mer students returned just to honor her?" She looked up. "Speaking of which, I just spotted our guest of honor arriving. I promised I'd escort her into the ballroom and see her to her table. I don't want her to be alone for even a minute."

Minutes later, as she linked her arm through her grandmother's, it occurred to Emily that her wor-ries had been groundless. Her grandmother may have decided to stop teaching, but her mind and her eyesight were as sharp as ever. Even without the name tags, their former teacher seemed to know the name of every person who walked up to her. It was obvious from the way Bert greeted them that she'd kept up with their lives. In many instances she knew where they lived and how they earned their living, as well as the names of their spouses and the numbers of their children.

Emily snagged a waiter and asked him to fetch their guest of honor a cup of tea after Bert rejected the suggestion of champagne. "I want to have a clear head tonight," her grandmother said in an aside. "I'll have my champagne later, when Frank and I are alone."

Emily was just turning back when she felt a hand at her shoulder and looked up to see the high-school custodian Albert Sneed. The mere touch of him put her on edge. Even when Emily had been a student, there had been something about Albert that had put her off. To the other students he'd seemed friendly enough, with silly jokes and a cackling laugh. But she'd never been able to warm to him. Even after all these years, she found herself thinking that his eyes seemed a little too hard, his manner a little too sly.

"Thought I'd offer my best to Mrs. B."

She managed a smile. "That's nice, Albert. She'll appreciate the fact that you came to see her."

"It's fun seeing all the old faces, Doc. So many of you pretty girls grew up to be pretty women."

Before she could reply she felt a hand on her

arm and looked over to see Prentice smiling down
at her. "Hello, Prentice. How's Will feeling?"

"Much better, thanks to you. I'd like to show
my appreciation. Can I get you a drink?"

"No, thanks. I have some things to see to."

"Okay. Maybe later. Thanks again, Emily. It's
always nice to get Will calmed down."

"You're welcome." Emily took a step back. "If
you'll excuse me, I have to get to the stage to
introduce our guest of honor. I hope," she added,
"you won't mind saying a few words to the as-
sembled."

"If you'd like."

"I would."

"Then consider it done."

She started toward the stage before she realized
that in the confusion, Albert was gone. She could
have hugged Prentice for his timely distraction.

Emily sat beside her grandmother while former
pupils offered their words of praise. First on the
stage was Robeson Ryder. A skilled orator whose
father had been a projectionist at the local movie
theatre, Robeson's words stirred the audience as he
talked about the teacher who had helped shape his
ideals, and how those ideals had now taken him to
a very public arena. He was a man who had dined

with presidents and kings, but retained a sense of humility that was appealing. He had an amazing presence, handsome and proud without a trace of arrogance. His voice was a deep rich baritone that could move the crowd to tears or to cheers.

By the time he turned the stage over to Prentice Osborn, Robeson Ryder had the audience on its feet cheering him.

Prentice was no slouch at working the crowd, either. He had them laughing, nodding in agreement and applauding as he told funny stories about himself and his days as a pupil of Mrs. Alberta Brennan. Even his old teacher laughed aloud.

When he was finished Emily strode to the microphone. "Thank you, Robeson, Prentice. Our little town is privileged to have two such famous sons."

From her position on stage she caught sight of a figure at the back of the room. For the space of a heartbeat the crowd seemed to melt away. All she could see was that face from the past. A strong chiseled jaw and lean handsome features. Those dark poet's eyes meeting hers and holding her gaze when she tried to look away.

She had to swallow before she could go on. "We have another celebrity in our midst. I wonder if Jason Cooper, bestselling author, would care to say a few words about his former teacher.''

It seemed, to Emily's ears, that there was a collective sigh sweeping through the room as the tall figure clad in a dark suit made his way to the stage, though there were a few, she noted, who hissed with annoyance. His book had stirred up strong feelings both of admiration and resentment in their town.

Jason didn't so much walk as stalk, glancing neither right nor left as the crowd seemed to part for him.

Emily set the microphone on the stand and moved to the far side of the stage, folding her hands together and hoping she didn't appear to be watching too closely as Jason Cooper climbed the stairs and paused center stage.

True to form, he seemed abrupt, edgy, as he picked up the microphone and said, ''I came here to honor Mrs. Brennan, who saw something in me all those years ago that I hadn't even seen in myself.'' He turned away from the crowd and stared at the old woman who was watching him so avidly. ''Whatever success I enjoy, Mrs. B, it's because of you. You changed my life, and for that I'll be eternally grateful.''

He set the microphone back on its stand and

strode down the steps, pausing beside his old teacher to press a kiss to her cheek.

Bert was beaming with pride. As Jason walked away, Emily thought she saw her grandmother wipe a tear from her eye.

She stepped to the microphone. "My grand-mother has asked me to thank all of you for coming tonight. We hope you can stay for our week-long celebration, which will include a garden luncheon sponsored by the alumni association, an original play entitled *An Orchid for Mrs. B,* sponsored by the high school, and a chance for individual visits with her throughout the week. Our celebration will culminate in a banquet and fireworks next weekend."

There was more applause before the crowd started to surge forward to surround not only the guest of honor, but also the celebrities who had spoken on her behalf.

Emily watched as Robeson and Prentice were engulfed in waves of people eager to shake their hands. While they worked the crowd, Jason beat a hasty retreat toward the exit.

Emily picked up her beaded bag and headed for the door of the now-empty ballroom. She'd stayed behind to check with the head of catering about the next day's luncheon in the Harbor House gardens. Satisfied with the details, she was flushed with pleasure. Especially since the weatherman was cooperating. There wasn't a trace of rain in the forecast.

She made her way through the lobby, hearing the sounds of voices and laughter coming from the bar, and stepped out onto the porch. As she crossed to the stairs a figure stepped out of the darkness beside one of the pillars.

"Oh." She caught her breath and brought a hand to her throat in a gesture of surprise. "Jason. You startled me."

"Sorry." He'd removed his jacket and tie and unbuttoned his shirt at the throat. His hair was slightly ruffled from the night breeze. In his hand was a tumbler of pale liquid. "I was just having a nightcap." At her lifted brow he amended, "Just soda. My father's legacy left me with no taste for alcohol. Join me?"

"No, I…" She froze when he stepped directly in front of her.

"We didn't get a chance to say hello in there." He was staring at her with that same dark, intense look that had always had the ability to do strange things to her heart. "Stay a minute, Emily."

It was on the tip of her tongue to refuse. But all

the years of anger and anguish, of fears and tears, dissolved when he looked at her that way. Besides, wasn't he the reason for the killer dress? Why waste it? "I suppose I could spare a few minutes."

He indicated the glider tucked away on one side of the porch, away from the winking lanterns. "The waiters have quit serving out here for the night. But if you'll wait there I'll get you a drink at the bar. What'll you have?"

She shrugged. "The same as you."

Minutes later he returned carrying a second glass and sat down beside her. After handing her a drink he touched the rim of his tumbler to hers. "Here's to Mrs. B."

Emily smiled in the darkness. "To my grand-mother."

They sipped in silence.

Emily leaned back, enjoying the slight motion of the glider. "She was so happy to see so many former pupils here tonight. But I think she was happiest to see you."

"What makes you think that?"

"I saw a tear in her eye after you spoke."

He shrugged, clearly uncomfortable. "It came from my heart."

"I know. That's what made it so special for her.

You didn't have any agenda. You weren't here to sell your books.''

He gave a sound that might have been a laugh or a sneer.

"Congratulations on your success, Jase." Emily wasn't even aware that she'd reverted to his old nickname. But he was. At the sound of it he went very still. "I always knew one day you'd find your life's calling."

"Yeah. You and Mrs. B. You two knew more than I did. I figured by this time in my life I'd probably be in jail. Or dead."

"You were never a troublemaker, Jase. You were just troubled. There's a difference."

"I wish you'd told that to the cops who routinely picked me up just for walking down the street."

Emily sighed. "Yes. You and Robeson, as I recall."

"At least he knew why he was being singled out. It was the color of his skin. As for me, I guess they figured with a father like mine, I was a likely suspect. If there was any trouble, they came looking to see if I had an alibi."

"It was so unfair."

He heard the temper in her voice. It was something he'd never forgotten. That hot sultry voice that could cool by degrees whenever she got angry. "It's just the way it was, Emily."

"But I still get angry thinking about it."

"Don't." His voice was barely a whisper. "It was a long time ago. It doesn't matter anymore." He turned to her. "I heard about your father. I'm sorry. Carrie said you came home and took care of him until he passed away. That couldn't have been easy."

She found herself marveling at the way he'd smoothly changed the subject. "Even healthy my father was…difficult. The stroke added to his frustration. But I'm glad I made the decision to come home. Though he never said so, I could see that he was pleased. And when he asked me to consider staying on for the sake of his patients, I agreed. At least for a while."

"So the move home isn't permanent?"

She shrugged. "I haven't decided. I'm taking it a day at a time."

"That's how I've taken every day since I left Devil's Cove." He drained his glass and set it aside. "One day at a time."

"I was worried sick when you left." The words were out of her mouth before she could stop them. She took a deep breath and decided to plow ahead. "Every day I figured I'd hear from you. And every day that passed was worse than the day before. Finally I started to believe that you'd be found dead hundreds of miles from here. You have no idea what you did to me by leaving without a word.''

The silence stretched between them, and she realized that he had no intention of explaining. Even after all these years.

She felt like a complete fool. ''I'd better go. I have an early appointment tomorrow.'' She got to her feet and turned away to set her half-empty glass on a wicker table. When she turned back, she found Jason standing directly in front of her, staring at her with such intensity, her heart took a quick bounce.

''I'll walk you to your car.''

She started past him. ''There's no need. It's parked at the curb.''

''Emily.'' He put a hand on her arm. Just a touch, but she felt the heat as surely as though she'd been held to a flame.

He turned her, keeping his hands at her upper arms as he drew her close enough to kiss. And though it was her intention to order him to stop, she couldn't speak. In truth, she wanted this every bit as much as he did. The thrill of anticipation shot through her.

He kept his eyes steady on hers as he lowered his lips to hers. Just a butterfly brush of mouth to mouth at first, testing, tasting. Then with a murmur of approval he took it deeper, until her lips warmed, softened, parted. He saw her lashes flutter, then close. Felt the way her breath came out in a sigh, filling his mouth with the taste of her.

He could feel the tension in her as he moved his hands slowly across her shoulders, down her back, drawing her closer, then closer still, until her body was imprinted on his. Her perfume was something light as spring rain. He drank her in, letting the taste, the scent, the feel of her, seep into his pores.

She felt like heaven in his arms. And tasted like sin.

Though she itched to touch him, Emily kept her hands firmly at her sides. If she felt a sudden rush of heat and her focus became blurred for a moment, she forced herself to remain perfectly still until her composure returned. And if the world seemed to tilt at a crazy angle as he deepened the kiss, she patiently waited until it settled.

He lifted his head and kept his hands at her shoulders, as much to steady himself as her. He was aware that she hadn't reached out to touch him. But he'd felt the way she'd trembled when they'd come together. It gave him a measure of satisfaction to know that she hadn't been as unaffected by their kiss as she let on.

"Good night, Emily."

"Good night." Her voice sounded breathy in her own ears, and she hoped he didn't notice.

On legs of rubber she made her way across the porch to the steps. The walk along the pathway to her car seemed like the longest she'd ever taken.

She had the strangest sensation that someone besides Jason was watching her. Someone standing in the shadows. She quickened her pace. Once in the car she turned on the ignition and fastened her belt, then put the car in gear and started down the street. On the wheel, her hands were sweating.

She touched a trembling finger to her lips. It occurred to her that David's kisses had never had this effect on her. In fact, in her whole life, no one's kisses had ever affected her like this.

No one but Jase.

But nothing could ever come of it. There were too many years and too many secrets between them.

Jason stayed in the shadows, watching the car's taillights disappear along the darkened street.

The door to the old inn opened, spilling light onto the porch. A burst of laughter announced several couples who'd been drinking at the bar. They never even noticed him as they hurried past him down the sidewalk toward a nearby bed-and-breakfast.

He heard a rustling of footsteps near the porch, but could see no one, and dismissed it as an animal.

As silence settled once more, Jason crossed his arms over his chest and leaned his back against the pillar, deep in thought.

When he'd walked into the ballroom tonight and caught sight of Emily on stage, it had been a tremendous jolt. Even though he'd been mentally preparing himself for that moment, he'd felt as though all the air had been squeezed from his lungs. He'd seen her so many times in his dreams. Yet the dreams couldn't hold a candle to reality. The years had added to her beauty. She was slimmer now, no longer a girl but a woman. The dress she'd worn had displayed every line and curve to her best advantage. Her hair was shorter now, falling just to her shoulders. When it had brushed his knuckles, it was every bit as soft as he'd remembered.

Then there was her taste. Sweet, yet laced with a hint of tartness. Emily Brennan had always been full of surprises. Despite her easygoing nature, there'd been a willful streak in her. A fierce independence that sometimes took a walk on the wild side. Her friends had recognized it. So had her father. Dr. Christopher Brennan had feared it, with good reason. Emily had a fondness for picking up strays. What else could account for her choice of friends? Though her father was a wealthy, successful doctor, she refused to hang out with the children of equally wealthy, successful businessmen in the town. Instead she chose to be with Jason and their friends, Carrie and Cory Lester, Robeson Ryder and the rest of the strange assortment of misfits who'd clung together through four years at Devil's Cove High.

Odd, he thought, how much they'd all changed. Cory, the wild man, was now an air force captain, Carrie the mother of a ten-year-old. And Robeson had found a healthy, legitimate outlet for all that anger.

Jason glanced at his watch. It was time he turned in. He had a full day planned tomorrow. He'd promised to go to Carrie's place to meet her daughter.

As he stood, he felt the hairs at the nape of his neck bristle, and sensed a presence nearby. He glanced around, but could see no one. Annoyed that he was letting his imagination play such tricks, he let himself into the hotel foyer.

He took the elevator to his floor and thought of his answer to Carrie's question this afternoon. He'd said then that he'd come back to Devil's Cove simply to honor Mrs. B.

He'd been fooling himself. Tonight, here on the porch in the darkness, he'd found his answer. The real reason why he'd come back. All it had taken was one kiss from Emily to get to the heart of the matter.

He'd come back to finish what they'd started all those years ago.

Chapter 4

"Hey, man." Jason clapped a hand on Robeson's shoulder. "You look like you could use a couple more hours of shut-eye."

The dining room of the Harbor House was bustling with people. The tables were dressed in starched linen cloths and crystal vases trailing ivy and fresh roses. The coffee was freshly ground, all the breads homemade.

"Long night." Robeson Ryder smiled. "Lots of old friends to get reacquainted with."

"Yeah." Jason's smile faded a bit. "I did a little catching up myself." And he had then spent more time than he cared to admit pacing his room last night, thinking about Emily.

He looked up when the young waitress approached. "Coffee. Black."

The smells coming from the kitchen made Jason's mouth water. "I washed dishes here one summer."

"You were one of the lucky ones." Robeson grinned. "They wouldn't let me near the kitchen. I got the job of mowing the lawn and pulling weeds. Did you know that we dug out each and every dandelion by hand? And if the groundskeeper found that we'd missed one, they docked our pay."

Jason laughed. "And we refer to them as the good old days."

"Maybe *you* do." Robeson drained his coffee and waited while the young waitress poured more. He looked over at Jason. "Ready to order?"

"Yeah. Bacon crisp. Eggs scrambled. Wheat toast."

Robeson shook his head. "Some things never change." He glanced at the waitress. "I'll have the same."

When she walked away he said, "So. Tell me about the writing biz."

"It satisfies my soul. And the pay's good. Now

tell me about life on the world stage as an advisor to the movers and shakers of our planet.''

Robeson wasn't surprised at his old friend's off-hand response. Jason Cooper had spent his entire childhood deflecting questions about himself. It was his armor against both shame and pain. Old habits, Robeson supposed, died hard.

He sipped his coffee. ''It no longer satisfies my soul the way it used to. I doubt the pay is as good as yours. And I can't sugar-coat the facts with a layer of fiction.''

They both laughed.

''Seriously.'' Robeson set down his cup. ''There was a time when it felt really good to find myself walking in the footsteps of some pretty great men. Not filling their shoes, mind you, but at least following where they led.''

''You've been leaving some pretty big footprints of your own, my friend.'' Jason shot him a quick smile. ''I've been following your successes. And they're damned impressive.''

Robeson shook his head. ''The way you and I were headed a few years ago, I never thought we'd be sitting here in the Harbor House, talking about our successes like old men.''

''I don't know. I should have seen your career as a rabble-rouser coming.'' At Robeson's snort of laughter Jason studied his old friend across the table. "Looking back on our high-school days, I seem to remember plenty of times when you managed to lead a student protest about something."

"Somebody had to do it."

"Yeah, but you took such delight in stirring up hornets' nests, and then watching everyone scramble for cover. Like the time Sue Bartlett wanted to compete on the wrestling team."

Robeson shrugged. "I was just ahead of my time. Now girls routinely join high-school wrestling teams."

"But the entire team threatened to quit if she was allowed to compete."

"That's only because she could kick their butts." Robeson chuckled. "Did you know that Sue's parents moved to Miller Falls? The high school there let Sue compete with the guys and she led them to a state championship."

"Sweet revenge. You were definitely ahead of your time, my friend."

Robeson laughed. "Maybe. Or maybe Devil's Cove was just out of step. Now maybe I'm the one who's out of step."

"What's that supposed to mean?"

Robeson stared down at his coffee. "I'm not sure I want to do this anymore."

"Can't stand success, huh?" Jason's smile faded when he saw the bleak look in his friend's eyes. "Hey, you're serious. What's this about?"

Robeson sipped, then set his cup down with a clatter. "It's not all champagne and caviar, Jase. Sometimes it's the threats against my wife and son. And sometimes it's the media watching me, hoping I'll slip and fall for the camera's glare."

"So you walk a little more carefully. And you hire bodyguards."

"Is that the way you'd like to live?"

Jason shook his head. "I'd hate it. But if that's the price you have to pay…"

"I could always walk away."

"And do what?"

Robeson shrugged. "There are at least a dozen law firms who'd pay dearly to add my name to their letterhead."

"You're more than a lawyer, Robeson. You know that. You have something special to offer this country."

"Not if I'm dead. Not if my reputation is ruined by some rag trying to dig up dirt."

Jason studied his old friend across the table. "Is there any dirt they can dig?"

Robeson gave a half smile. "I suppose if they

dig deep enough. I never tried to live my life like a saint.''

"Not as long as I knew you.''

They both laughed, then looked up when the waitress served their orders.

"One thing Devil's Cove can brag about is this place.'' Jason tucked into his meal and Robeson followed suit. "I'll bet you haven't found many places around the world that can bake better bread than right here in the Harbor House.''

Robeson nodded. "I was just thinking the same thing.'' He slathered wild strawberry jelly on a piece of toast and tasted. "Now if they added soul food to the menu they'd definitely be world-class.''

Both men laughed easily as they finished their breakfast.

Robeson took a last drink of coffee. "I've got to get going. I promised Mrs. B. I'd visit her this morning. Then we have that lunch here in the gardens. Afterward I'm doing an interview with a local news crew.'' He shoved back from the table and looked down at his old friend. "How about you?''

Jason shrugged. "I'm going to Carrie's to meet her daughter.'' He saw the quick frown on his friend's face. "You knew she had a daughter, didn't you?''

Robeson nodded. "Yeah. I heard. Well…" He clapped a hand on Jason's shoulder. "I'll see you at the luncheon."

With his jacket hooked over his shoulder by a thumb, Jason walked up the steps of a modest white frame house in a newer section of town that boasted street after street of similar homes. The lawn was neatly trimmed. White petunias framed either side of the porch.

The door was opened before he could ring the bell.

Carrie looked past him to the street. "Where's your car?"

"I walked."

"Jason, it's almost a mile from the Harbor House."

"I needed the exercise."

She studied the muscles of his arms visible beneath the knit shirt. "You look like you have a personal trainer."

"Thanks. But so far I've managed just fine on my own." He stepped past her into a neat living room. "I didn't see you at the kickoff party last night."

"The night waitress didn't show, so I had to work the next shift." She shrugged. "Not that I minded. I'd rather have the money in my envelope than make small talk with a bunch of strangers who never had anything to do with me when I was in school. Come on. I want you to meet Jenny.'' She led the way to the kitchen, where a blond freckled girl in a baseball uniform was seated on a stool, nibbling a peanut butter sandwich.

''Jenny, this is an old friend of mine, Jason Cooper.''

He walked over and took the stool beside her. ''Hi, Jenny.''

''Hi.'' The girl drank her milk and wiped at her mouth with the back of her hand. ''You in town for the tribute to Mrs. B.?''

''Yep. Is your school involved?''

She shook her head. ''Just the high school.''

''What grade are you in?''

''Fifth.''

''You like it?''

She shrugged. ''It's okay. My mom says you write books.''

''That's right.''

''What kind?''

''The kind with gory murders and creepy villains.''

''Wow. Neat. Did you bring a copy for my mom?''

"Yeah."

"Can I read it?"

"I don't think that'd be a good idea. Maybe you ought to stick to Harry Potter."

"Gram says they've got too much black magic in them."

"What do you think?"

"Nope. I like them." She looked up at the sound of a horn. "There's Mrs. Winston." She grabbed her baseball cap and pulled it on before racing over to kiss her mother's cheek. "See you in a couple hours. Wish me luck."

"Good luck. Drive one over the fence." Carrie tugged on a lock of blond hair. "Love you."

"You, too."

As her daughter raced to the door Carrie called, "Are you forgetting your manners?"

The girl turned. "Bye, Jason. Nice meeting you." Then she was gone.

"She's a great kid, Carrie. She looks just like you."

"You think so?"

"Yeah. And it looks like you're doing a fine job of raising her."

Carrie's smile grew. "She thinks I'm too strict. Isn't that a hoot? I broke every rule in the book, and spent more time in detention than anyone else in our class, and my daughter thinks I'm too strict.''

''Are you?''

She looked away. ''Maybe I'm too aware of the pitfalls. I just don't want her to get hurt, Jason.''

''Yeah. But you can't keep her in a bubble.''

Her grin was quick. ''I'd like to.'' She gave him a steady look. ''Wait till you have a kid someday. Then you'll understand.''

''I suppose you're right.'' He turned to watch as the little girl climbed into a van filled with half a dozen other girls.

Carrie picked up the plate and glass and set them in the dishwasher. ''Want something to eat?''

''No thanks. I just had breakfast with Robeson.''

''How did he look? I mean…'' She flushed. ''…does he look as successful as you?''

Jason shrugged. ''He looks satisfied with his life. I'd call that successful.''

She turned away to stare out the window. ''Did you see Emily last night?''

''Yeah.''

She turned back to study him. ''And?''

''And what?''

A little cat smile touched the corners of her lips. ''Try that with somebody else, Jason Cooper. I know you, remember?''

"Yeah, you do, Carrie. Probably better than most. In case I haven't told you, I appreciate all those letters keeping me up on things here in Devil's Cove."

"I was happy to do it. Especially when you'd write back. It made me feel like I was getting away from here, if only for an hour or so." She arched a brow. "I also know you well enough to know that you're very good at changing the subject. So, tell me. Did you and Emily talk?"

"A little. But not about anything important."

"Did she ask you why you'd left without a word?"

He nodded.

"And you didn't tell her?"

"No."

She rounded the kitchen island and stared at him more closely. "She deserves to know."

"Yeah." He caught her hand. "Come on. Let's go to the garden luncheon for Mrs. B."

She drew back. "I don't think so."

"Why not? Come on. It'll be fun. You'll see all those old classmates who used to snub you."

She winced. "Yeah. *That's* going to convince me to go. You'll have to do better, Jason."

"Okay. How about this." He tipped up her chin

so he could watch her eyes. "Robeson told me
he'd be there."

He saw her reaction and grinned. "My, my, Ms.
Lester. I believe you're blushing."

She slapped aside his hand. "And I believe you
haven't changed one bit. You still love teasing me
every chance you get."

"You got that right." He winked. "Just so you
know. It sounds as though he's happily married."

"I'm glad."

"Are you?"

She blushed again and said nothing.

"Are you coming?"

She started toward the hallway. "Just give me a
few minutes to freshen my makeup."

Emily arrived at the Harbor House, dressed in
what she always thought of as her lady clothes. A
knee-skimming sheath in seafoam silk with a
matching jacket. On her feet, simple taupe sandals.
At her throat, her grandmother's pearls, a gift on
her eighteenth birthday.

She told herself she'd arrived early because she
had to see to the last-minute details of the luncheon, but she knew that wasn't so. The catering
staff of the old inn routinely handled such affairs
with ease. By the time she made her way to the

gardens the tables and chairs had been set on the lawn. The florist had delivered dozens of baskets of colorful daisies to grace each table. A buffet was being set up under a colorful awning. The members of the high-school string quartet were setting up their instruments. Everything was moving along smoothly. There was really nothing for her to do but wait for her committee to arrive and begin directing the guests to their seats.

She glanced toward the upper windows of the inn, wondering which room was Jason's, then chided herself for such foolishness. She was acting like a high-school girl with her first crush.

That's what Jason had been. Her first love. And though there had been others, she'd never been able to get him out of her mind. Oh, she'd managed to get on with her life after he'd left town. She'd even managed to lock him away in a secret corner of her memory. She'd convinced herself that that was all he was. A bittersweet memory from long ago.

And now he was back in Devil's Cove, looking so much better than she'd remembered. Still dark and brooding and secretive. But stronger somehow. Even more commanding a presence. Did that come from success? she wondered. Or from traveling the world on his own terms? Whatever the reason, he'd made her feel the way she always did when a storm was brewing. Tense. Edgy. The very air around her heavy and oppressive. And she knew that if the rain came she'd want to walk in it, oblivious to the threat of lightning.

"Hey, Emily." Robeson's deep baritone broke through her thoughts as he dropped a hand on her shoulder. "You're looking awfully serious on such a pretty day."

"Robeson." She turned and flung her arms around his neck. "You were so mobbed by admirers last night we never even got a chance to properly greet each other."

"There's time now." He gave her a warm, affectionate hug. "We might even get time to talk over lunch."

"I'd like that."

"So would I. I brought your grandmother." He nodded toward a cluster of people surrounding their old teacher. "She's asked me to sit at her table. I hope you're joining us."

"I'd love to. The caterers have set up her table in the gazebo so it can be seen by everyone at the luncheon." She looped her arm through his and walked beside him. "I have to tell you, Robeson. Whenever I see you on TV I just feel so proud."

"Thanks." He grinned. "Of course, you and

Jase and Carrie had to listen to my litany of complaints long before the public heard them. I'll bet you didn't realize I was honing my skills on all of you.''

''Yeah. I think we all figured you'd go on to do some pretty great things with your life. We just never realized how quickly you'd climb to the top.''

He threw back his head and chuckled. ''It's a very tall ladder I'm climbing, Emily. I figure it'll take me a lifetime or two to get to the top.''

''But look how far you've gone already.'' She shook her head as they approached the gazebo where the guest of honor was already taking her seat. ''Advisor to the President. Consultant to kings and prime ministers. The media refers to you as the conscience of the world.''

Robeson patted her hand. ''I used to think if I was able to change just one bigot's conscience, it would be enough for me.'' He shook his head. ''But these days, I'm not so sure of myself.''

''What do you mean?''

He gave an expressive shrug of his shoulders. ''Nothing. Maybe I'm just getting burned out.'' He leaned close. ''Come on. Let's see what words of wisdom our old teacher will dispense today.''

They took their places across the table from Bert

and were quickly joined by Prentice Osborn and several members of the school board.

When Jason and Carrie arrived, Bert looked up with a bright smile. "Oh, Jason. Here you are. Come join us. And you, too, Carrie."

Emily saw the way Carrie glanced around wildly, hoping to escape. But it was too late. Everyone at the table was looking at her. Jason put a hand beneath her elbow and helped her to a vacant chair between Robeson and Prentice, before taking the seat beside his old teacher.

To put Carrie at ease Emily reached past Robeson to touch a hand to her arm. "How's Jenny?"

The mere mention of her daughter made Carrie smile. "She's fine. She has a baseball game today."

"What position does she play?"

"Shortstop. I always tease her by saying the shortest one on the team has to play that position."

That had the others laughing.

Robeson said, "As I recall you were a pitcher for our girls' team. A darn good one."

Carrie's smile bloomed. "I wasn't bad, was I? Except when you and Jason and Emily would come and watch. Then I got all flustered."

Emily glanced at her grandmother across the table, engaged in an animated conversation with Jason. "You were good enough that Bert thought you should try for a sport scholarship."

Carrie nodded. "It was a sweet dream. Until reality set in." She turned to Emily. "Speaking of dreams, Jenny said her class was invited to tour your clinic just before school let out for the summer. She came home filled with thoughts of becoming a doctor."

"Oh, that's wonderful. I was hoping that little tour might take some of the mystery out of medicine for the students. If it serves as an inspiration for future careers, that's all the better." Emily looked up to see that the others were watching and listening.

Her grandmother fixed her with a look. "Does this mean you've decided to stay on in town, Emily?"

Emily could feel Jason's dark look pinning her and was relieved when the head of catering approached and asked the guest of honor to lead her table toward the buffet line. As they shoved back their chairs and began to follow, Emily felt Jason's hand on her arm. There it was again. That quick rush of heat that was nearly overpowering.

He leaned close. "Do you have any plans for tonight?"

She shrugged. "I've scheduled a few patients."

"What time will they be gone?"

"Around seven."

"Good. Have dinner with me." He hated the urgency in his tone. It wasn't so much an invitation as a plea.

It was on the tip of her tongue to refuse. They'd said everything they had to say to each other last night. Nothing had changed between them. He was still as secretive as ever, refusing to give her any reason for his abrupt departure from the town and from her life. Besides, she reminded herself, she was still raw from that shattering kiss.

Maybe it was because of that kiss that her heart answered instead of her head. "Make it seven-thirty."

He smiled and pressed a hand to her shoulder.

It occurred to Emily that she was inviting trouble. But then, that was nothing new. She'd been in trouble from the first moment she'd heard that Jason Cooper was back in Devil's Cove.

Chapter 5

"Thanks, Mel." Emily set aside the phone and turned to the anxious couple seated across from her desk in the conference room. "Dorothy, you have an appointment for a CAT Scan at ten Tuesday morning at University Hospital. That was the earliest they could see you." She turned to the woman's husband. "Victor, you'll want to leave around seven. That way you can avoid traffic, and take the time to get there without any stress." She smiled gently. "There's been enough of that in your lives."

The gray-haired man drew an arm around his wife's shoulders as she got weakly to her feet. Before they reached the door Emily was there, holding it open.

She was startled to see Jason standing in the outer office, chatting with Melissa. He looked up and for one brief moment she felt her heart hitch at the look in his eyes. Then she returned her attention to the elderly couple beside her.

"Don't be anxious about the scan, Dorothy. It's noninvasive. It won't hurt."

"That's good to know. Thank you, Dr. Brennan."

Her husband nodded. "Dorothy and I appreciate all you've done." He added with a sigh, "I wish you were coming with us."

Emily laid a hand over his. "Don't let the size of the place overwhelm you. University Hospital is big but not impersonal. I know Doctor Liu. He's one of the best. He'll take really good care of Dorothy."

When they were gone, Emily's assistant snatched up her purse and started toward the door. "I'm late. Ben phoned to say he has supper waiting. I'll see you Monday." She dimpled at the man across the room. "Nice seeing you, Jason."

"You, too, Mel."

When she was gone Emily glanced at the clock. "Sorry. I thought I'd be finished an hour ago."

She began unbuttoning her lab coat. "I can be changed in minutes."

"Take your time." Jason nodded toward the door. "Maybe I'll poke my head in the kitchen and say hi to Trudy."

That had Emily grinning. "Who do you think you're fooling? You're just hoping to find a plate of chocolate chip cookies, aren't you?"

"Guilty." He winked, and she felt her heart do a series of somersaults as she started away.

As Jason made his way along the hall toward the kitchen, it warmed him to see that little had changed. The same decorative tiles that had reminded him as a boy of Aztec art he'd seen in a history class. The same cherry cabinets, polished to a high shine, some with leaded glass fronts showing off fine china and crystal. Hardwood floors gleaming in the last rays of sunlight streaming through arched cathedral windows. To one side, on a Turkish rug of gold-and-green and ivory stood an enormous trestle table, its only adornment a simple bowl of apples. Across from the sink was a work island topped with a slab of gold-and-green-veined marble.

Trudy was lifting something from the oven when she caught sight of him. For an instant she merely stared. Then the smile came. First to her eyes, and then to her mouth.

"Well, aren't you a sight. Mrs. B. told me you were back, Jason."

He glanced at the tray of cookies in her hands. "Did you bake those for me?"

"Don't you wish?" She gave a rusty laugh. "The judge still has to feed his sweet tooth every night."

"I'm surprised Mrs. B. allows it."

"She pretends not to know." The old woman set down the plate and gave him a long steady look. "You've been missed."

"By you, Trudy?"

"Me and…" She merely shrugged. "…others."

He was across the room in quick strides and brushed a kiss over her wrinkled cheek. "Thanks."

"For what?" As he straightened she touched a hand to the spot, as if to hold the warmth of it.

"For not changing." He picked up a cookie and broke it in half, watching the chocolate ooze.

"That's what you think. Change is good." She studied him as he took his first bite. "Maybe I haven't changed, but you have."

"How?"

"I've followed your success. We all have. It looks good on you."

"Thanks. And you think that's changed me?"

She shook her head. "You got yourself some polish."

At that he managed a deep-throated laugh. "Much needed, I'm sure."

"I don't know." She sank down onto a cushioned armchair at the head of the table. "I always thought all those rough edges looked good on you."

"Careful, Trudy." He finished the last bite and gave her a dangerous smile. "I could lose my heart to a woman who not only bakes my favorite cookies, but gives compliments in the bargain." He got down on one knee in front of her. "Will you marry me?"

She slapped his arm. "You were always crazy."

"Crazy about you." He met her steady gaze. "It felt strange coming back."

She leaned forward. "Good strange or bad strange?"

He shrugged. "I haven't figured that out yet."

Her tone lowered. Softened. "Been by your old house yet?"

"No need." He got to his feet and, restless, began to prowl the kitchen. "Strangers are living there now. I hope they're happier than I was."

He knelt to pet the cat that dozed on a corner of the rug. "One of Emily's strays?"

Trudy nodded. "Some things never change. If it were up to her we'd be running a zoo. I always figured she'd doctor animals instead of people." She watched him resume his pacing. "I heard your ma passed away."

"More than a year ago."

"Where'd she go after leaving Devil's Cove?"

Jason paused at the French doors, hands clasped behind his back. "Chicago. She had a sister there."

"Did she know about your success?"

He made a sound that was not quite a laugh. "She never said." He pointed to a sailboat dancing along the shoreline. "Look at that, Trudy. Now there's something I never got tired of seeing when I was a kid."

She got slowly to her feet and crossed the room to stand beside him. "Probably heading up to Mackinac Island."

He hooked a thumb in his back pocket and rocked back on his heels. "Did you ever just want to climb aboard one of those and leave the world behind?"

"Don't like water." Trudy shivered. "Especially big lakes. I like to see what kind of slimy things are swimming under my feet."

"Where's your sense of adventure?"

She chuckled. "It went the way of my waistline."

As she stood watching the sailboat skim out of sight she realized Jason Cooper hadn't changed as much as she'd first thought. Even as a boy he'd been very good at deflecting attention away from himself with a simple question, a diversion. Whatever it took. Hadn't he just done it again?

Before she could ask him anything more, Emily stepped into the kitchen, and the atmosphere in the room was suddenly charged with electricity. The housekeeper looked from Jason to Emily, seeing the nerves just beneath the careful smiles.

He eyed the pale linen slacks and the silk blouse the color of watermelon. "That didn't take you long."

"I told you I'd only be a few minutes." Emily spotted the plate of cookies. "Good timing. How many did you manage to eat?"

"Just one." Jason winked at Trudy before crossing to take Emily's arm. "If the judge leaves any, I might have a nightcap later."

"My advice is to take all you want now." Emily

shared a laugh with the housekeeper. "If Bert leaves Poppie alone for even a few minutes, that plate will be empty."

Trudy nodded. "Emily's not kidding. The judge has been known to eat an entire batch at one sitting."

"Then I'll leave him to it." Jason paused. "Thanks for the sweets, Trudy. Maybe I'll see you later in the week. I'm hoping for a nice, long visit with Mrs. B. before I head back."

"I'll look for you." She was already fumbling for the pack of cigarettes she kept in her pocket.

As soon as Jason and Emily were gone, the old woman stepped out onto the patio and lit up, inhaling deeply. She knew it irritated Dr. Emily to see her smoking, just the way it had irritated the elder Dr. Brennan. Trudy had endured all their lectures and had quietly gone about doing what she always did. Whatever the consequences of her actions, she'd face them when the time came.

She heard the purr of a car engine, and listened as it moved down the long curving driveway. In the silence that followed she caught sight of another sailboat far out on the lake and found herself thinking about what Jason had said.

To a boy who'd endured hell, she supposed a boat to anywhere would have seemed heaven-sent.

Still, now that he'd finally achieved his freedom, he'd returned.

It would take a powerful need to bring him back to a place with such unhappy memories. Was it a need to pay tribute to his old teacher? she wondered. She exhaled a wreath of smoke and watched as it dissipated into the air. Or was she right in thinking it had nothing whatever to do with Mrs. B. and everything to do with Emily?

Old Dr. B. would turn over in his grave.

"Where are we going?" Emily studied Jason's hands on the wheel of the rented Porsche. Such big hands. They suited him. Strong. Capable. With enough strength to snap her bones if he chose. And yet she could still recall them holding her with such tenderness.

"I made a reservation at the Pier."

"They don't take reservations except for parties of six or more."

"Really?" She saw his lips curve into a smile. "They didn't tell me a thing about that. Just took my name and said they'd hold a table."

"Must be nice to have that kind of clout."

"It has its moments."

She studied his profile in silence.

He glanced over. "Do you always keep such late office hours?"

"This was an exception. One of those medical mysteries that will require endless tests before we know what we're dealing with."

"Your patient looked scared."

Emily nodded. "She has a right to be. Actually, Dorothy seems resigned to whatever the tests find. I think she's anticipating the worst. It's her husband I'm worried about. Victor is expecting a miracle."

"Then I hope he gets it."

Emily sighed. "I hope so, too. But I don't like the odds."

They drove through the heart of downtown, where throngs of pedestrians browsed the antique and gift shops and spilled out into every available space in the restaurants and outdoor cafés.

Jason's voice was warm with humor. "I hope the businessmen of Devil's Cove remember to thank your grandmother for luring all her old students back. Or is business always this good?"

Emily laughed. "Devil's Cove is thriving, as I'm sure you've noticed. But I've never seen this many people in town at one time."

He found a parking space and maneuvered the little sports car to the curb before rounding the

hood and holding her door. As they crossed the
street and headed toward the pier that jutted into
Lake Michigan he caught her hand. A simple gesture, but she couldn't ignore the quick rush of heat
as their fingers linked.

At the far end of the pier was a converted ware-
house that was now one of the town's most fash-
ionable restaurants. People crowded the wooden
benches on either side of the front door. Inside
Emily and Jason had to wade through even more
people who milled about the bar area, awaiting
their tables. There was a festive atmosphere, and
nobody seemed to mind the wait, as drinks flowed
and voices were raised in laughter.

The minute Jason gave his name to the hostess
she picked up two menus and led them to a private
booth at the window, overlooking the water.

Emily felt Jason's hand skim her back as he held
her chair. Again, just a touch, but it was enough
to have her tingling from the contact.

He took the seat across from her and smiled at
the waitress who hurried over to take their drink
orders. Minutes later he was drinking iced tea
while Emily sipped cool, pale chardonnay and
waited for her heartbeat to settle.

Jason glanced at the ball of orange sun that

seemed to be riding the crest of waves far out on the horizon. "I've never forgotten these sunsets."

"You mean you don't have something even more spectacular in Malibu?"

He smiled. "We probably do. I just never take the time to notice."

"I guess a career like yours would keep you awfully busy."

"No more than yours." He gave her a long, steady look. "Your dad must have been proud."

She flushed. "I suppose. He never said."

"He didn't need to. You came back and took care of him after his stroke, didn't you? And when he asked you to stay on, you did." His tone deepened. "I'm not surprised, Em. For all your rebellion, you were your father's daughter."

"Really?" She gave a short laugh. "I wish you'd told me that years ago. It would have spared me a lot of energy I spent on rebellious mistakes."

"A wise person once told me there aren't any mistakes. Every choice we make is just another lesson to be learned. Every step, no matter how faltering, brings us closer to our ultimate goal."

She worried the rim of her wineglass, running her index finger around and around. "Then I've had more than my share of lessons and steps."

"I know what you mean." He caught her hand,

stilling the movement. "I'm an expert on the high cost of learning."

This time as they looked at each other across the table, their smiles came easily.

"Tell me about the places you've been and the things you've done, Jase."

He looked down at her hand in his. "I don't think we have enough time to cover all of it. Let's just say I saw most of the country, and I've tried my hand at just about everything from shoveling manure to rubbing shoulders with the rich and famous."

"And now you're one of them."

He gave a grunt of laughter.

"Did you have a goal, or were you just running?"

"Running. As far and as fast as I could."

"But you ended up writing." Her voice took on a dreamy note. "Bert always said you would. She and I have devoured all your books."

He wasn't prepared for the little jolt of pleasure her words brought. "That's nice to hear. I'm glad, Em."

When their waitress appeared to take their order, Emily withdrew her hand and picked up the menu, scanning and ordering quickly. Jason did the same.

When they were alone again Emily sipped her wine. "There's a lot of darkness in your books."

"There was a lot of darkness in my life." He grinned suddenly. "I guess they'll never be mistaken for romances."

They shared an easy laugh.

"The murders in this latest book are pretty brutal." Emily paused a heartbeat before adding, "There's a rumor going around town that the setting is a thinly-disguised Devil's Cove."

For a moment she thought he might not respond. She saw his quick frown before he shrugged. "This town was always good at rumors. But…" Before he could say more, a shadow fell over their table.

"I heard you were back, Cooper."

They both looked up at the stocky man who stood, legs apart, hands clenched at his sides, rocking back and forth on the balls of his feet.

"Boyd." It took Jason no more than a moment to place the former classmate who had once been an all-state quarterback on their high-school football team. Now the lean face had filled out and gone to jowls. The athlete's body had thickened around the middle.

Jason started to shove back his chair, but a beefy

hand on his shoulder stopped him. "You come back here to gloat, Cooper?"

Jason shrugged aside the hand and got to his feet so that his eyes were level with the intruder's. "I came back to thank a teacher who made a difference in my life." He took a long look at the police uniform and the badge pinned to the man's chest. "I see it's Chief Thompson now. You took up where your father left off, did you, Boyd?"

"You got that right. And I don't like anybody suggesting he didn't do his job."

Jason's eyes narrowed. "What's that supposed to mean?"

"Your new book. Everybody's saying it pokes holes in my father's handling of those murder cases all those years ago."

"If you read the book, you'd know it was fiction."

"Is that what you're calling it?" Boyd's chin jutted. "You might be some big important literary hero in that new life you made, with more money than you'll ever need. But here in Devil's Cove, we still remember what you really are. My father was right about you all those years ago. You're nothing but the town drunk's bastard."

Jason saw the way heads turned at Boyd's angry outburst. Though his face remained impassive, his voice barely a whisper, the blaze of white-hot fury in his eyes had the sheriff backing up a step. "If you're thinking you can still arrest me for that, the way your father did, you'd better go home and study the law."

"I'll go home when I'm good and ready."

"You might want to explain yourself to the manager who's heading this way."

As the chief spun away, Jason leaned close to whisper, "But you were right about one thing, Boyd. All that money I'm making can buy me some damned fine lawyers."

He stood watching as the uniform was swallowed up in the crowd at the bar. When the waitress appeared with their food, Jason sat down quietly and studied Emily across the table.

Neither of them spoke, allowing the hum of voices in the background to fill the silence.

At last Jason took her hand in his and managed a thin smile. "Nice to know some things never change."

"That was hateful. But then, Boyd Thompson was never known for his pleasant personality."

"How did he manage to inherit the job of police chief after his father retired?"

"It's been in their family a long time. Besides…'' She shrugged. ''As near as I can gather, nobody else wanted it.''

Jason looked down at his plate and squeezed her hand before releasing it. ''No sense letting all this food go to waste.''

So many questions swirled around in Emily's head, but she was reluctant to spoil another moment. And so she followed his lead and simply ate her meal in silence.

Later, as they took their leave of the restaurant, once more Jason caught Emily's hand. This time he thought he'd prepared himself for the quick jolt, but it still managed to take him by surprise.

''Let's stroll along the pier. I need to walk off all that food.''

''Good idea.'' Emily absorbed the heat that raced along her arm. ''I couldn't even make a dent in the salad, the lake trout, the twice-baked potato. But then you had to tempt me by ordering the crème brûlée topped with fresh strawberries.''

He chuckled in the darkness. ''I didn't force you to eat it.''

''You didn't have to. It's a weakness of mine. When it comes to dessert, I have absolutely no willpower.''

''Hmm. Interesting.'' He leaned close. ''What are your other weaknesses, Dr. Brennan?''

She pressed a hand to his chest. "As if I'd tell you."

Laughing, he turned to watch the play of harbor lights on the water. "This is one of mine."

"Mine, too." She didn't even know she sighed. "I like it better in the fall, though, when the tourists are gone. Sometimes I'm the only one out here, and I find myself wondering where all the big boats are headed."

He leaned a hip against the wooden rail. "That was my favorite game when I was a kid. I'd imagine myself sneaking aboard one of them, going to some exotic port in the South Pacific."

"You always wanted to get away from Devil's Cove. And now you've done it."

"It wasn't the town I wanted to leave. Or you, Emily." His voice roughened. "Never you."

"But you did. Without a word."

"I know. I'm sorry about that. You'll never know how…" His head came up sharply, glancing left, then right.

Emily touched a hand to his arm. "What is it?"

He shrugged. "Just a feeling. Like someone is watching us."

Emily studied the half dozen couples strolling in the moonlight. Along the far rail an old man was fishing, his hamper beside him.

"I don't see anyone who seems even vaguely interested in us."

A breeze sent their hair dancing and whipped the waves to froth. Seeing Emily shiver, Jason drew an arm around her shoulders. "Come on. I'll get you home."

By the time they'd walked to his car, the shops were closing, the streets empty except for the few tourists still searching for a restaurant or bar.

They rode slowly through the town while Emily brought Jason up to date on her family.

"Courtney studied interior design in New York and Milan, then came back here to open a shop. She lives above it. Sid's an artist now, living in a cottage near the old lighthouse. Hannah's nursery and landscaping company is just starting to take off. And my mother's real estate firm was just selected to represent the new golf course and harbor development."

"Sounds like life is good for the Brennans."

She nodded, then fell silent as she caught Jason checking the rearview mirror several times as they headed toward the historic district. When they came to The Willows, he turned the Porsche onto the tree-lined drive.

When they came to a stop he opened her door

and kept her hand in his as they walked up the steps of the front porch.

"I never expected to be doing this." He waited while she turned a key in the lock and shoved the door open. "How does it feel to be living here again?"

She turned to him. "Not as strange as I'd feared. I fought it at first. But once I was here, I realized it wasn't like being a kid again. I'm here on my own terms. The house is big enough that we're not tripping over each other. I can see my family if I choose to, or be by myself when the mood strikes."

He closed a hand over her shoulder and leaned close. "You mean, if I were to spend the night in your room, nobody would notice?"

She laughed. "Sorry. The house isn't that big."

"Too bad." In the moonlight her dark hair seemed dusted with diamonds. He had a desperate urge to touch it. "It might have been fun."

"I doubt I'd risk it for fun. Memorable, maybe. Spectacular, possibly." She shook her head and there was a teasing light of laughter in her eyes, eyes that glinted brighter than the stars overhead. "As a writer I'd have expected you to come up with something much more descriptive than *fun.*"

"You're right. What was I thinking?" He thrust

both hands into her hair and nearly sighed from the pleasure. It was as soft as he remembered. And her mouth was absolutely made for kissing. "I give you my solemn promise. If you invite me up to your room we'll spend a night of a thousand pleasures, all of them beyond the description of mere mortals."

She was laughing as he lowered his mouth to hers. It was the merest brush of mouth to mouth, but the laughter died in her throat. Her lashes fluttered, then closed as he took the kiss deeper and she lost herself in it.

The ground beneath her feet seemed to shift and she reached out blindly, clutching his waist to keep from falling.

"Did that change your mind?" He kept his mouth on hers, whispering the words against her lips. And though he strove for lightness, there was the slightest edge to his voice.

Her only response was a hum of pleasure as her lips softened, opened, inviting more.

He needed no other invitation. His arms came around her, molding her to the length of him while he kissed her long and slow and deep until their hearts were thundering and they were both gasping for air.

He looked down at her hands fisted in the front of his shirt. "Is that a yes?"

She was surprised at how difficult it was to laugh over the dryness in her throat. "Sorry. I'm still planning on sleeping alone."

"That's what I was afraid of." He brushed a last kiss over her lips and drew away. "Sweet dreams."

"You, too."

She stood in the doorway and watched as he returned to the car and put it in gear. As the headlights moved down the driveway, she stood very still, waiting for her heartbeat to return to normal.

What was it about Jason Cooper? With nothing more than a kiss, he still had the ability to make her feel like a lovestruck teen.

Whatever it was, she thought as she headed toward the stairs, it was even more powerful now than when they'd been high-school sweethearts.

Chapter 6

In front of the Harbor House, Jason stepped from the car and handed the keys to the valet. As he made his way up the walkway he couldn't shake the feeling that he was being watched. But the few people standing on the porch seemed to take no interest in him as he passed, and by the time he reached the front door he was chiding himself on his wild imagination. The curse of a mystery writer, he supposed.

The moment he stepped inside the lobby the night clerk snatched up a book from under the counter and hurried over. The young man glanced around nervously before holding out the book.

"We were warned not to bother you, Mr. Cooper, but I was wondering if you'd mind signing this."

Jason grinned. "I don't mind a bit." He accepted a pen and flipped open the book. "What's your name?"

"Mark Sobiesky. But Mark will do."

Jason scrawled his name. "You go to school, Mark?"

The boy nodded. "Michigan State. I'll be a junior in the fall."

"What's your major?"

"Journalism."

"You hoping to write?"

"Yeah. I'd love to do what you do. I've read all your books." The young clerk accepted the pen and book almost reverently. As he turned away he called, "You rock."

"Thanks." Jason was still grinning as he turned away and caught sight of Robeson's head in the bar.

He approached the booth and found his old friend enjoying a drink with Prentice Osborn.

"Hey." Robeson looked up and slid over to make room. "Join us, Jase. What'll you have?"

Jason nodded toward the mug in his friend's

hand. "Not what you're having, I'm afraid. Coffee, I guess."

"Coffee," Robeson called to the bartender.

Minutes later Jason touched his cup to their glasses and took a moment to drink.

"Out catching up with old friends?" Robeson dipped a hand in the bowl of chips.

"Yeah. How about you?"

Prentice didn't give Robeson time to answer. "He was just telling me he stopped by the Daisy Diner."

"For old times' sake," Robeson was quick to add.

"Was Carrie working tonight?"

Robeson gave a slight nod before ducking his head.

Across the table, Prentice was shaking his head. "You're the only man I know who, after being interviewed by CNN, passes up a gourmet dinner at the Harbor House to eat at the local diner."

"Why not?" Jason gave a friendly nudge of his elbow. "I hear they have great grilled cheese sandwiches."

"And the waitress happens to be an old friend." Robeson was determined to defend himself against the inevitable taunts.

"Who happens to look sexy in that uniform and

apron.'' Jason's eyes danced with unconcealed humor. ''You always had a thing for uniforms, didn't you? I remember that girl in ROTC. What was her name?''

''Justine Gack.'' Robeson shook his head. ''I saw her yesterday, with her husband and two sons. Nature hasn't been kind to Justine.''

''Sorry to hear that.''

''I bet her husband's even sorrier.''

That had the three men laughing easily together.

''Speaking of uniforms. Our local police chief paid a nasty visit to my table in the Pier to warn me that I was on his hit list.''

Robeson's smile was quickly wiped away. ''Don't tell me our football hero has become the same kind of pain in the ass his father used to be.''

''Looks that way. He seemed to be itching for a fight. He went away disappointed. I wouldn't give him the satisfaction.''

Robeson sipped his beer. ''Don't mess with him, Jase. He might be a jerk, but remember, he's got the law on his side.''

''I'll remember.'' Jason looked over at Prentice. ''What did you do tonight?''

''This and that.'' He gave a negligent shrug of his shoulders. ''Like you, old friends to catch up with.''

"I hear you're selling off some of the family property."

"A developer made me an offer I couldn't refuse."

Jason studied him over the rim of his cup. "You don't mind that your family estate keeps shrinking more each year?"

"Not as long as it makes me a millionaire in the process."

Robeson gave a snort. "I thought your grandfather did that before you were born."

Prentice nodded. "My grandfather was a smart man. He said only a fool would put his money in stocks when he could put it in land. But my father wasn't listening. By the time he died the estate was nearly bankrupt."

Prentice drained his drink. When he looked up his smile was back. "I'd better run. Carrie's mom is with Will. She'll want to be getting home."

Robeson arched a brow at Prentice's mention of his handicapped brother. "You can't leave Will alone?"

"I do when I have to. But I prefer to have someone there with him. He gets…agitated when he's alone."

"Agitated? Has he ever done damage?"

"Only to himself. He's clumsy. He's fallen

down the stairs a couple of times. And slipped in the bathroom.'' Prentice slid from the booth and offered a handshake. ''I guess I'll be seeing you two around in the next couple of days.''

They called their good-nights, and Jason took the seat vacated by Prentice.

''It's got to be hard taking care of a brother like Will.'' Robeson nursed his beer. ''I have to give Prentice credit for that. He could have had Will put away in some expensive institution and nobody would have faulted him for it.'' Robeson studied his friend. ''I don't think you're even listening to me. What's bothering you?''

Jason grinned. ''Maybe it's coming back here and remembering why I was so eager to get away. That run-in with Boyd Thompson didn't help.'' He drained his coffee and got to his feet. ''I think I'll turn in now.''

As he started away Robeson called, ''Have you had a visit with Mrs. B?''

''I'm seeing her in the morning.'' With a wave of his hand he walked away.

After stepping into the ancient elevator he punched the button. Despite some creaking, it moved smoothly and came to a halt at the third floor, where he stepped out and crossed the hall to

his room. As he let himself in, he was thinking
about Emily in her room at The Willows.

Hours later, when he finally shut down his computer and turned in for the night, he was still thinking about Emily. There was no denying that the
years they'd been apart hadn't dimmed the magic
between them. If anything, it was stronger than
ever.

"Jason." Before he'd even stepped from his car
Bert was standing on the front porch to greet him.

"Mrs. B." He kissed her cheek and kept her
hands in his as she stepped back to study him.

"You look so good, Jason. You've made a good
life for yourself?"

He nodded. "Thanks to you."

"Nonsense. You'd have found your way regard-
less."

"Maybe." His smile was quick and warm. "But
it didn't hurt to know I had a champion on my
side."

"Come in." She turned and led him through the
pretty foyer. Instead of taking him to the parlor,
she veered toward the kitchen. "As soon as Trudy
heard you were coming, she got busy making all
your favorites."

"I didn't want any fuss."

She paused and laughed. "Tell that to Trudy."

"Tell me what?" The housekeeper was just walking in from the patio, wiping her hands on her apron.

Jason breathed in the wonderful aroma of citrus and spice that filled the air. "I didn't want you to fuss, Trudy."

"I'm not fussing." She waved a hand at the two of them. "Go out and enjoy the sunshine. I made iced tea."

Jason followed his old teacher to the patio and glanced around. "Where's the judge?"

"Puttering in his workroom. He'll be along soon. Unless he forgets to eat, which often happens when he's lost in a project."

"Still inventing?"

Bert nodded as she took a seat on a glider and invited Jason to sit beside her. "It keeps him from missing the courtroom."

"What'll you do to keep from missing a classroom full of students?"

She laid a hand over his. "Maybe I'll take up the piano."

That had them both chuckling.

She sighed. "I'm sure I'll feel a pang or two when September rolls around. But it'll be nice to know I can come and go as I please. It was time to walk away, before they had to carry me off.''

''Will you be shopping for a retirement home in some warmer climate?''

She crossed her arms and stared out at the water, dotted with boats. ''I don't think I could ever leave here. I'd miss all this too much.''

''You could always come back in the summer.'' He followed the direction of her gaze. ''The town's growing.''

''It is, but not so much that it's jarring.''

''Would you ever sell The Willows?''

''Why do you ask? Are you thinking of buying it?''

He merely grinned.

She shook her head. ''I hope I can live out my life here. But if I can't…'' She shrugged. ''I'd like to think one of my family would remain here. Speaking of family, were you surprised to see Emily living and working here?''

''Yeah.'' He gave a short laugh. ''I couldn't believe it when I saw her named as chairman of the tribute committee.''

She gave him a sideways look. ''And that's when you decided to attend the reunion.''

''You always knew me too well.''

''It took a while. You were very good at keeping

secrets. I guess that's why I decided to look beyond the face you showed the world.''

"I'm glad you did."

"So am I." She reached for the sweating glass of iced tea and sipped. On the far side of the patio, Trudy was busy setting lunch on the glass-topped table. "I enjoy your books, Jason. They're gripping. The minute I start reading, I forget you wrote them."

"That's the finest compliment you could pay me."

"This latest book was terrifying." She lowered her voice. "I suppose you realize you've ruffled a few feathers here in Devil's Cove."

He gave her a bland smile. "Is that so?"

She sighed. "I remember the murders. They happened years ago, but most citizens remember them well. The authorities agreed that they weren't connected."

"*If* my book was about Devil's Cove, and *if* I had been chronicling actual crimes, I'd have to point out that the authorities don't have a very good track record. Of the two convictions, one was later overturned by an appeals court, and a second man died proclaiming his innocence. A third murder went unsolved, as I recall."

"In your book you suggest a serial killer. One who could still be alive here in our town."

He chuckled. "If my fictional town were really Devil's Cove."

"Yes, of course." He was still very good at secrets, she decided. Once he made up his mind, there was no budging Jason Cooper.

When Trudy beckoned, Jason got to his feet and put a hand under Bert's elbow. They both looked up as Charley and Sidney stepped onto the patio.

"Jason." Charley's pleasure was evident in the smile that seemed to brighten all her features as she crossed the distance between them and gave him a warm embrace. "Oh, don't you look grand."

"Thanks." He turned to accept a hug from Sidney, whose smile matched her mother's. "I think you were sweet sixteen the last time I saw you. Now you look even more like your mother."

Sidney dimpled. "That's quite a compliment."

He turned to Charley. "I see your name on just about every piece of property in this town."

"Oh. There are a few choice properties I've missed." She laughed. "But I'll admit I've been busy."

While they stood and caught up, Frank Brennan and his granddaughter Hannah walked up, heads bent in animated conversation. When they spotted Jason they both hurried over to welcome him.

Frank shook his hand. "You're looking good, son."

"Thank you, sir. So are you." Jason turned to Hannah. "And you're all grown up."

"But still a tomboy." She indicated her torn jeans and ragged fingernails. "This morning I was working with my crew laying sod because two of my employees didn't show up."

"Hannah owns a landscaping company." Her grandfather's pride was evident in his tone.

"I've seen the signs on just about every pretty garden in town."

While they talked, they gathered around the table where Courtney joined them.

"Hello, Jason." She offered her hand and he couldn't help admiring the smooth, polished look of her.

"Em said you studied in New York and Milan. It shows."

"Thank you, I think. Is that meant as a compliment?"

"You bet. You're all grown up, and even prettier than I remember."

Trudy unloaded platters from a wheeled serving cart. Just as they were taking their places, Emily stepped out the door. She'd removed her lab coat and was wearing a simple skirt and blouse. When she saw Jason with her family she paused for half a beat.

Bert glanced at the man beside her and saw the look of pleasure in his eyes. Then she looked over at her granddaughter. Even from this distance the electricity between these two was almost palpable.

After a moment's hesitation Emily managed a smile. "Well, this is a surprise. Nobody mentioned that you were coming for lunch, Jason."

Bert busied herself with her napkin. "I guess I forgot to mention it. When Jason phoned and asked to visit, I found I had a few hours free today."

Emily gave her grandmother a considering look. "I thought you had a hair appointment at the Harbor Salon."

"It was canceled."

Emily decided not to press the issue. But she would have bet a week's pay that her grandmother had been the one to cancel it when she learned that Jason wanted to come calling.

"Sit here, Jason." Bert took her usual place at the far end of the table and patted the chair beside hers, so that Emily was wedged between him and her sister Sidney.

As soon as they were seated, Trudy began serving.

After helping himself to fish from a platter Jason looked up with a grin. "I thought you said you didn't fuss."

Trudy showed no emotion. "I didn't."

Jason winked at Hannah across the table. "I suppose this is your usual fare? Broiled lake trout? Tomatoes vinaigrette? Lighter-than-air-biscuits?"

Bert answered for her. "The judge has always been fussy about food. And he prefers his main meal at noon rather than later in the day."

"You have excellent taste, sir."

"Thank you, son." Frank tucked into his meal. To no one in particular he announced. "I invented a new spatula today."

Trudy rolled her eyes.

Frank ignored her. "It folds over like a sandwich, to keep from dropping the food as you turn it. And each side is vented to allow the juices to escape while turning meat or fish on the grill."

"I think that's been done," Bert said dryly.

"Not like this one. The handle is long enough to use on the hottest outdoor grill."

The housekeeper paused beside him. "I'm surprised you didn't tuck a Swiss army knife into the handle, so you could slice, dice or drill the meat or fish while you're at it.''

He shot her a scathing look. ''You may poke fun now, but you'll thank me after you've had a chance to try it.''

''When will we get to see this latest ingenious invention?'' Trudy replaced the platter on the cart.

''I should have it refined and ready to use by tomorrow.''

''Which means,'' Hannah said in a stage whisper, ''that Trudy will probably manage to misplace it by the end of the week.''

The others around the table were grinning.

At Jason's arched brow, Emily said softly, ''Trudy doesn't have the heart to tell Poppie how much she hates his inventions, so she just manages to lose them.''

''And he's never caught on?''

Emily shrugged. ''He's the quintessential absent-minded professor. As soon as he finishes one project, his mind is on the next, and he completely forgets what went on before.''

Trudy, busy topping off their iced tea, muttered, ''One of these days you'll invent something I can use. Like an apple corer that doesn't leave those jagged holes in the middle. Or a grapefruit spoon that actually cuts through grapefruit.''

''Careful.'' Bert touched a hand to the housekeeper's arm. ''If he should take your advice, you
may have actually to use one of his inventions.''

Trudy nodded. ''And then I'll never hear the end
of the man's brilliance.''

''Brilliant, you say?'' Frank looked up with a
gleam in his eye. ''Thank you, Trudy. Nice of you
to finally acknowledge that fact.''

Jason sipped his tea and managed not to laugh
out loud. It felt so good to sit back and watch again
the bantering and bickering that he'd first wit-
nessed as a boy. He'd learned early on that, despite
the litany of complaints between these two, there
was a deep well of affection. It flowed not only
from Frank Brennan to Trudy, but from person to
person around this table. So much love, given
without reservation. When he'd first encountered it
he'd felt like a cave dweller emerging for the first
time into the warmth of the sun. At first it had
merely dazzled him. Then it had led to compari-
sons between the blinding light of this life and the
dullness of his own existence. Finally he'd realized
that he could never again be content to leave the
warmth behind and crawl back into the darkness.

This was why he'd left Devil's Cove.

This was why he'd returned.

Chapter 7

Bert touched a napkin to her lips and studied Jason as he watched the antics going on around him. The look on his face left no doubt that he was enjoying himself.

She could still recall the sad, somber boy who had followed Emily into the kitchen one soggy summer day. He'd been as bedraggled a stray as any of the animals her granddaughter had rescued. More so, perhaps, because he was so heartbreakingly stoic. When she and Trudy had discovered the marks and bruises on his body, he'd had an excuse for every one. A fall from a bike or tree. A tumble on the sidewalk. A scrape from a passing boat.

Was that when he'd begun weaving fact into fiction?

"Got to run." Hannah pushed away from the table. "The sod truck ought to be rolling up with another load any minute. Thanks, Trudy. That was great." She waved to Jason. "I hope I see you again before you leave."

Before he could respond she was gone, and the others were on their feet, ready to follow.

Charley checked her watch. "I have a one o'clock showing." She kissed Bert's cheek, then the judge's before offering her hand to Jason. "So good seeing you."

It was Sidney's turn for goodbyes, followed by Courtney, and then the judge, who was eager to return to his workshop.

Frank Brennan offered a firm handshake to their guest. "Nice to see you, son. I'm sure we'll get together a few more times before the week ends."

"I hope so, sir." Jason returned the handshake.

Emily brushed a kiss over her grandmother's cheek. "I have patients waiting." When she turned, she nearly bumped into Jason. At once his hands were on her arms, steadying her. She stood perfectly still for a moment, enjoying the quick rush of heat that accompanied his touch. Reluctantly she turned away.

He stood watching as she crossed the patio and stepped through the open French doors.

If Bert had had any doubts before, they'd been swept away in that instant. The looks on both their faces had been achingly revealing.

She cleared her throat. "She's grown into a lovely young woman, hasn't she?"

Jason blinked and realized he'd been caught staring. He held out a hand and helped her to her feet. "You're a sly woman, Mrs. B."

"So I've been told." She tucked her arm through his. "Walk with me, Jason. It will give us a chance to catch up."

They left the patio and followed weathered stepping stones set in the lawn leading down to the water's edge. There they stood watching the play of watercraft.

"My son, Christopher, was a strong-willed man."

Jason chuckled. "I wonder where he got that?"

She joined in his laughter. "I guess he was his mother's son. But he also inherited his father's keen sense of duty. As the father of four daughters, he was determined to give them every opportunity to have the futures he thought they deserved."

"What if they wanted a life he didn't approve of?"

The old woman crossed her arms over her chest and faced into the breeze. "I think he really believed he could persuade them to want what he wanted. As you well know, he was not above pulling strings to get his way."

Jason stuffed his hands in his pockets and studied the white sails in the distance.

"I don't know what Christopher would make of Sidney's secluded cottage in the woods, though he always sensed she would have a future in the arts. It was as natural to her as breathing. He probably would have preferred that she live and work in one of the great cultural centers, like Paris or Rome, or even New York. As for Hannah's tomboy career as a landscaper, he would probably disapprove, consider it unladylike. I'm sure he'd have nagged and cajoled and even lobbied to get her to simply design the gardens, and leave the physical work to others. Not that she would have listened to him. Our Hannah has a mind of her own. And I believe he would have approved of Courtney studying in Milan." Her tone softened. "Of course, his untimely death left such questions without answers."

Jason heard the pain in her voice. It must have been devastating to have lost her only child. "You haven't mentioned Emily. Her choice, at least, would have pleased him.''

Bert turned, and her smile was forced. ''My son was a good man, but he wasn't above using even his impending death to his advantage. It should have been enough to know that Emily had followed him into medicine. He knew, from all accounts, that she was headed for a brilliant career at University Hospital. But he extracted her promise to remain here, at least until she could find a worthy replacement.''

''You think he was wrong to ask that?''

''I thought so in the beginning, and said as much. Now I'm not so certain. When Emily first returned to Devil's Cove, she seemed eager to get back to the life she'd made for herself. Her own apartment. Her friends. Her hectic schedule. Not to mention a certain doctor who was taking up a great deal of her time.'' Bert saw the narrowed look that came into Jason's eyes and nearly laughed aloud. Oh, he was so transparent, though he would have vigorously argued that point with her. ''But in the weeks since, I've watched Emily shrug off the tensions that go along with such a life. She's actually begun to blossom, in ways I hadn't expected. I think she likes being closer to her family, and reestablishing relationships with old friends.''

"And her brilliant future?"

"If she wants it, I believe it's still hers for the taking. But success, by itself, isn't all that satisfying, as I'm sure you've learned. There are other things that need to be taken into account." She took his arm and began to walk along the shore. "Tell me about your life, Jason. You're living in California now?"

"Malibu."

"Do you jog along the beach and ogle movie stars?"

He roared with laughter. "I do. But I try not to be too obvious about the ogling."

"Have you made friends there?"

"A few."

"Tell me about them."

"There's a director who's been wrangling with studio executives to turn my work into movies. He can be pretty persuasive when he tries. We started out with a few lunches and meetings, and discovered that we like the same things and enjoy the same company. He and his wife are fun to be around. And there's my agent and her husband and kids. They make me feel like part of their family."

"That's good. You need family, Jason." Bert gave him a sideways glance. "How about romantic entanglements?"

"Is that a polite way of asking me if I have a roommate?"

It was her turn to laugh. "I believe it is."

"Mrs. B, you're losing your touch. That was about as subtle as a train wreck."

She stopped walking and looked up at him. "You haven't answered the question."

"It doesn't deserve an answer." He couldn't suppress the grin that curved his mouth at her little huff of impatience. "All right. You win. No roommate. No significant other."

"Why?"

"Because you broke my heart all those years ago, and no other woman could measure up."

She smacked his arm before linking hers and continuing along the shore. "I'm trying to have a serious conversation here."

"So am I. But the beautiful woman on my arm is distracting me."

They walked in silence, enjoying the loveliness of the afternoon and the ease with which they fell into their old relationship of teacher and pupil, with even amounts of lecturing and teasing.

Bert's tone softened. "She was hurt when you left without a word."

Jason had no problem keeping pace with the sudden change in the conversation. "I know. I've always been sorry about that." *Sorry*. Such a mild term for the way he'd felt. As though his heart had been pulled from his chest and trampled in the dirt until it was bloodied and shredded into hundreds of pieces. The pain of separation from Emily had been harder than the pain of his childhood. But he'd survived. They both had.

"Christopher was surprised by your strict code of honor. Of course, I took every chance I could to remind him that I'd expected as much."

Jason paused to look down at her. "When I came to you for advice, you told me that I should take every opportunity that was handed me, no matter how many strings were attached. As I recall, you told me that one day I'd look back on all that with a sense of pride." His tone roughened. "Where's that one day you promised me, Mrs. B?"

"You don't have a sense of pride in your accomplishments, Jason? What about your success? Your celebrity?" Seeing his frown she added, "Your books are bestsellers. Your face, your name splashed on the covers of magazines. Your lifestyle noted among the rich and famous. There aren't many of your classmates who would turn down the chance to trade places with you."

"I can't deny that I like what I've done. Writing

satisfies a need in me. I like the discipline of it.
The challenge. And it certainly helps that my pub-
lishers are willing to pay me so much money for
doing what I love.''

"But…?''

He took her arm and started back the way they'd
come. From here The Willows, with its graceful
sloping roof and fabulous gardens looked like an
exotic picture in a slick magazine. "But something's missing.''

"Is that all?'' There was a sparkle in her eyes
that reminded him of another. "Think of your life
as a puzzle, with a key part missing. You were
always so good at finding what was lost, Jason.''
She saw Trudy standing on the patio, a wreath of
smoke drifting over her head. "Come on. Let's get
back to the house and see if there's any iced tea
left. Maybe Emily can join us between patients.''

"You're a devious woman, Mrs. B.''

She laughed. "Thank you. I like to think so.''

Emily stepped out of the examining room and
made her way to Melissa's desk. "No more patients?''

"Hank Carver canceled. So did Emery Mi-
chaels. That leaves an empty hour in our schedule,
which is handy, because your grandmother asked

if you'd see her on the patio when you found some time."

Emily laughed. "I guess that means I can't use this hour to deal with the mountain of paperwork on my desk."

"I've seen that mess. An hour wouldn't even make a dent."

Emily sighed. "You're right, Mel. I guess we both know what I'll be doing on my next day off." She started toward the door, unbuttoning her lab coat as she walked.

She passed Trudy in the front foyer, polishing an antique cabinet that served as a coat closet. In the kitchen the dishwasher was humming. As she stepped out onto the patio, she saw her grandmother and Jason seated on the glider, heads bent in quiet conversation.

The sight of them together did something strange to her heart.

They both looked up and saw her at the same moment. Jason was on his feet and helping her grandmother to stand before they both hurried across the patio to greet her.

"Emily." Bert kissed her granddaughter's cheek. "I was hoping you'd find time for another visit, but I never dreamed it would be so soon."

"Two cancellations in a row." Emily grinned.

"I'm learning that this is the life of a small-town doctor. Too many patients and not enough time, and then sudden holes in the schedule that leave me feeling oddly disconnected."

"Your father used to love those unexpected cancellations. He claimed they gave him enough time to fish a dozen nearby streams."

Emily burst into laughter. "I'd forgotten that." She turned to Jason. "Dad used to carry his fishing gear in a black bag similar to his medical bag. He used to stow both in the trunk of his car. One day he was flagged down by a man whose wife had gone into labor."

"Milt Levender," her grandmother added.

"That's right. Dad reached into his trunk, grabbed his bag and hustled into the Levenders' bedroom. When he pulled out a tackle box, and Milt caught sight of all those lures and hooks, he fainted on the spot. Poor Dad had to run back out to his car, exchange the fishing gear for his medical bag and hustle back inside to deliver a baby."

Bert took up the story. "By the time Milt came to, his wife Deb was lying in bed holding their brand-new son in her arms. To this day, Milt and Deb credit Christopher with their son Eric's love of fishing. I believe Eric won the annual trout competition three years in a row."

Jason was laughing as he turned to Emily. "So, are you thinking of taking up fishing, too?"

"Not a chance. I wouldn't have the heart to put the worms on the hook."

"You could bring Hannah along for that."

She shook her head. "It wouldn't do any good. I'd just have to toss the fish back in the lake anyway."

"Or bring them home and make pets out of them," Bert said dryly. She patted her granddaughter's arm. "If you two will excuse me, I'll be back in a few minutes."

She walked away, leaving them alone.

Jason nodded toward the pitcher on the glass-topped table. "Want some iced tea?"

"Sounds good." Emily moved along beside him and watched as he poured a glass of tea. He handed it to her before topping off his own.

Instead of taking a seat she walked to the edge of the patio and looked out over the water. Jason paused beside her.

"Did you and Bert have a nice visit?"

He nodded. "She seems to think you might stay in Devil's Cove."

Emily shrugged. "I hope she doesn't pin too much hope on that. I honestly don't know how I'll feel a month from now. A year. Or even tomorrow.''

''I think whatever you decide will be just fine with your grandparents.''

''There's something to be said for having so much family. If I go, they'll still have my mother and sisters to fill their hours.''

''Who will you have to fill yours, Em?''

She stared into her glass with a frown. ''I could ask you the same thing.''

When he didn't say anything she turned to glance up at his face. She'd expected him to be laughing, or perhaps mocking. Instead, what she saw in his eyes was a look so bleak, it twisted a knife in her heart.

She touched a hand to his arm. ''What are you doing for dinner tonight?''

''Having dinner at the Harbor House with Robeson. Join us.''

When she started to shake her head he set aside his glass and closed a hand over hers. ''We have a lot of years to catch up on. And so little time. Say yes.''

Emily fought to ignore the curl of pleasure at his touch. ''All right. But you and Robeson may have to start without me. My last appointment is Mrs. Crenshaw, and she's always late.''

He bent close and pressed a kiss to her brow. "You'll miss the best gossip."

Her hand tightened on his arm. "Don't you dare talk about anything juicy until I get there. Promise?"

She saw the way he studied her mouth, inches from his, and felt the heat.

They both looked up when they realized Bert was standing in the doorway, watching them.

Jason stepped back a pace. "Promise."

When the older woman walked up, he paused to brush a kiss over her cheek. "Thanks for the lunch, Mrs. B. And the conversation. Both were even better than I'd remembered."

"I'm glad. Will I see you again, Jason?"

He nodded. "You bet."

The two women were silent until he was gone.

Emily drained her glass and glanced at her watch. "I'd better get back to the clinic. Before I go, what did you want to see me about?"

"See you?"

Emily nodded. "Mel said you wanted to see me."

Bert shrugged. "Whatever it was, it must not have been too important. It seems to have slipped my mind."

Her granddaughter gave her a speculative look. "Nothing ever slips your mind, Bert."

"I'm an old woman. These things happen."

"The last time you admitted to being old was when you wanted to con Poppie into hiring a limo for your birthday. What's your con this time?"

"You offend me, Emily. Can't I simply crave your company?"

"Uh-huh." Emily gave a throaty laugh. "You're up to something, Bert."

The old woman turned away. "I think it's time you got back to work."

"You're right." Emily brushed a kiss over her cheek and started away. Over her shoulder she called, "Tell Trudy I won't be here for dinner tonight. I'm joining Jason and Robeson at the Harbor House."

"I'll tell her." Bert was smiling as she picked up the empty glasses and headed toward the kitchen.

It had been a very productive afternoon. She'd had a lovely visit with a young man she really liked. She'd had a chance to see for herself that the magic was still there between him and her granddaughter. And she'd managed to get those two young people together again. If they hadn't spotted her, she was pretty sure they'd have kissed right here on the patio.

She had a feeling tonight would take care of itself.

Chapter 8

Emily knew she was taking too much care with her dress. She'd changed three times. The first, a black jersey, had been too bland. The second, a bold print, too colorful. Now she slipped a simple red silk sheath over her head and felt it glide over the dips and curves of her body in one fluid sweep. She decided it was just right. Sexy without being revealing. And proper enough, if she ran into patients, to keep them from going into cardiac arrest. That thought brought a smile to her lips. But, she decided, the hair was all wrong. She pulled one side off her face, fastening it with a jeweled comb, and added blood-red teardrop earrings before standing back to study her reflection.

She should have taken a pass on dinner tonight. She was treading on dangerous ground with Jason. He'd already hurt her once. If she allowed it to happen again, shame on her. But she wouldn't permit it, she thought with a fierce shake of her head. She was a smart woman. Smart enough to graduate number one in her class at Michigan, and to compete against the best and the brightest at Georgetown before taking up residency at University Hospital. This was nothing more than a dinner date with an old school friend. If they enjoyed a little flirtation, what was the harm? She'd keep it simple.

She wasn't going to sleep with him.

There. She smiled at her reflection. Now that she had that out of the way, she would simply enjoy the evening.

She turned and picked up a small handbag, tucking in her cell phone and pager along with her wallet and keys.

The entire family had gathered in the dining room. The judge and Bert, her mother and sisters, were already seated at the table, with Trudy standing beside the judge's chair. The two were arguing about something, as usual.

Emily paused in the doorway.

"Big date?" Sidney smiled as she looked over.

"I'm joining Jason and Robeson Ryder at the Harbor House."

"Killer dress," Hannah said with a grin.

"You think so?" Emily struck a pose, her hand on her hip.

"Yeah. If I ever have a hot date, I'd like to borrow it."

"It's yours." Emily blew her family a kiss and turned away. "Don't wait up."

The dining room of the Harbor House was bustling with activity. Waiters in crisp white shirts and black pants, most of them college students home for the summer, made their way through the crowds. Candles flickered invitingly in low bowls of roses and peonies that adorned each table. On the enclosed patio a piano player entertained with show tunes.

"In a lot of ways Malibu is like a small town." Jason sat back in the half-moon banquette, enjoying a spirited disagreement with Robeson that felt amazingly like old times. It occurred to him that they hadn't bonded all those years ago because they'd both been outsiders, but because they'd fed off each other's strong opinions. It had been the same with Emily.

His head came up sharply, sensing her even before he caught sight of her. He spotted her threading her way toward them, and was instantly on his feet.

Robeson glowed with pleasure as he caught her hand. "I'm so glad you were able to join us."

Emily felt the brush of Jason's hand at her back as she took her seat. She wasn't surprised at the way her body reacted, the quick skitter of heat along her spine, the way her heart lurched ever so slightly. Still, it was disconcerting. Was she going to have this reaction every time he touched her?

There was such heat in his eyes when he looked at her. As though he could devour her on the spot. It had the blood pounding in her temples.

She sucked in a breath and turned to Robeson. "You're sure you don't mind the intrusion?"

Robeson settled himself on one side of her, with Jason on the other. "You could never be an intrusion, Emily."

She dimpled. "I don't know. You two seemed awfully deep in conversation."

Robeson grinned at Jason. "We were on our favorite topic."

"Politics?"

Jason shook his head. "Women."

Emily wrinkled her nose. "I thought you would have outgrown that by now."

"A man never outgrows his appreciation for women. Especially beautiful women. It's something in the genes." The way he said it had her cheeks coloring.

She strove to keep the atmosphere light. "I should have known."

When a waiter hurried over, Emily ordered a drink. Minutes later she sipped cabernet and found herself in the middle of a debate between her dinner partners on the advantages of living in a bustling urban area after a childhood in Devil's Cove.

"I hated everyone knowing my business." Robeson watched as a waiter placed a tray of appetizers on their table. "When I was a kid here, even the grocer knew when we couldn't pay our bills."

"But at least he let you buy on credit." Emily helped herself to a curried shrimp. "My father probably knew everyone's business, too, but he kept what he knew to himself. And he continued to treat their illnesses with kindness and compassion, even if they couldn't pay. Would you find that in a big city?"

Jason laughed. "Emily makes a good point. What do you say to that?"

Robeson shrugged. "It's true that there may be some advantages to small towns. But you can't deny that you hated everyone knowing about your father, Jase."

"Of course I did." Jason nodded. "But I think no matter where we live, it's impossible to hide dirty little secrets for a lifetime. Sooner or later they get out."

Emily set down her fork. "I know one secret you managed to hide from your friends for a number of years."

He arched a brow. "And that would be?"

"That you had a talent for writing. I don't recall you ever writing anything memorable while you were in school." She turned to Robeson. "Do you?"

Robeson thought for a moment. "As I recall, Jase once wrote a piece for the *Devil's Cove High Scribe,* in which he detailed the science lab disaster that had the entire student body scrambling to escape the stench of rotten eggs."

Emily's eyes sparkled. "I'd forgotten that. He wrote the entire piece like science fiction." She turned to Jason and, without thinking, grabbed his hand. "What did you call it?"

He absorbed the warmth of her touch and managed a grin. "'The Slime That Ate Devil's Cove.'

I don't know how you could have forgotten. It was illustrated by your sister Sidney. That might have been, in fact, a turning point in her career. She drew the entire thing like a really bad comic book. It was the talk of the school.''

"Sid probably has a copy of that somewhere in her portfolio. I think she's kept everything she ever drew.''

Jason chuckled. "I'll have to ask her next time I see her. I might want a copy for myself, in case my publisher rejects my next book proposal.''

"Fat chance.'' Robeson set his menu aside. "I think half the people in the airport were reading your latest.'' He lowered his voice. "And I'll bet half of them were trying to figure out if it was based on fact, or was just a figment of the author's wild imagination.''

"Are you ever going to tell us?'' Emily sipped her drink. "Or is there a stipulation in your contract that forbids you from discussing your research?''

Robeson grinned. "Maybe the rumors are true, and Jase has uncovered a serial killer right here in town.''

Instead of the expected laughter, Jason picked up his menu and began to scan it.

Robeson reached over, snatching the menu out of his hand. "What kind of an answer is that?"

Jason managed a thin smile. "I write fiction, Robeson. You know that."

"Right. But your fictional town was too close to Devil's Cove to have been an invention. And I don't hear you denying that your story bears an uncanny resemblance to that string of crimes that happened here." He gave his friend a long, steady look as he handed him back his menu. "Do you know something we don't?"

Jason set it aside. "The authorities said the murders were unrelated."

"But you think they were?"

He gave a shrug of his shoulders. "It doesn't matter what I think. I'm a writer of fiction. That gives me the freedom to solve the crimes to my own satisfaction, and move on."

"So, this wasn't something you uncovered in your research?"

"I'll admit that I was given access to a lot of information. I read files that have been closed for years. But in the end, I was left to draw my own conclusions."

"And this was just your take on something that happened here a long time ago?"

Jason nodded, before turning his attention to the waiter who took their order.

When the waiter was gone Emily saw Robeson staring at a woman across the room. She turned to him. "Someone you know?"

He shook his head. "For a minute I saw the blond hair and thought it was Carrie." He seemed to consider for a moment before adding, "I asked her to join us for dinner, but she said she had to work."

"That's too bad." Emily smiled at him. "I would have enjoyed her company. The four of us used to have such fun together, didn't we?"

Robeson gave a thoughtful nod before signaling the waiter for another drink.

"Do you remember the time we took the judge's boat out after midnight and ran out of gas?" Emily's eyes crinkled with the memory. "Jase and I were the strongest swimmers, so we left you and Carrie in the boat with the flashlight, while we swam to shore."

Jason chuckled. "You were the one who persuaded me to wake up Red Hanson and ask him to loan us a tank of gas and his boat."

Emily started laughing. "Red was so mad. How was I to know he'd just filled a prescription for sleeping pills because he was having his tonsils out the next day?''

''Your bright little scheme cost me a month of working after school every night without pay for Red's father in his garage, just to make it up to him.''

''I don't know what you're complaining about. Didn't I bring you pizza and a bag of Trudy's chocolate chip cookies almost every night?''

''Yeah, you did.'' Jason smiled at the memory of stolen kisses in the back of Hanson's Garage, which were even sweeter than Trudy's cookies.

When he glanced across the table, Robeson seemed to have gone somewhere in his mind as he sipped his drink. When he realized he'd been caught he set down his drink with a clatter. ''You think working for Red's father was bad, you should have seen Carrie's mother when I got her home. I'd have gladly changed places with you rather than face that woman's wrath. I'll bet even after all these years she'd still like to tan my hide.''

''I haven't seen her since I got here, but I met Carrie's daughter.'' Jason paused while their waiter placed their meals in front of them. When he was gone, Jason added, ''She seems like a great kid.''

Emily nodded. ''Jenny and her classmates had a

field trip to my clinic for career week. She asked some really bright questions. Carrie said ever since then she's been showing an interest in the field of medicine.''

"Good for her.'' Jason turned to Robeson. "How old is your boy?"

"Three."

Emily's eyes lit up. "I hope you brought pictures."

"Yeah." Robeson fumbled in his pocket for his wallet and produced a photo of his wife and son. "This is Anthea and Robeson, Jr."

"She's beautiful." Emily passed the picture to Jason. "And your son looks just like you."

Robeson's smile returned as he studied the faces in the photo before returning it to his wallet.

Emily smoothed her napkin. "Why didn't they come with you?"

"They're with relatives in Atlanta. Anthea talked about leaving Roby with them and joining me here, but I didn't want her to have to change her plans, so I came alone."

"Next time bring them along," Emily said as she began to eat.

"Yes, ma'am." Robeson winked at her before tucking into his meal.

A short time later Jason saw their waiter heading toward their table. "Anybody want dessert?"

Emily shook her head. "What I'd rather do is have coffee out on the patio and sing along with the piano player."

Robeson started laughing. "You know she's going to con us into singing along, too, don't you, Jase?"

"Yeah." Jason winked at her. "You were always good at conning us into going along with your schemes, Em."

"And if I recall, despite all your protests, you always ended up enjoying yourselves. Come on." When the bill was paid she walked arm-in-arm with Jason and Robeson toward the raucous guests who were singing show tunes. "You'll have a good time if it kills you."

The two men shared a knowing smile as they said in unison, "Yes, ma'am."

The last tinkling notes of "Summertime" filled the air as waiters moved about the patio picking up empty glasses. The few diehards who had remained to the end began drifting inside as the piano player stuffed music sheets into a briefcase and hurried away.

An hour earlier Robeson had said good-night,

leaving Emily and Jason seated at the piano bar. After singing along with the others, they'd danced in the moonlight. Nobody noticed as they stood, swaying softly in the shadows, dipping, gliding, until their movements had slowed, then stopped entirely. They'd stood, watching each other with hesitant smiles, before retreating to an arbor where they sat breathing in the wonderful perfume of roses that grew in glorious tangles around them.

Jason set aside his empty coffee cup. "This used to be a great make-out spot in our high-school days. Remember?"

Emily's voice was warm with laughter. "We foolishly believed the teachers didn't notice all the couples slipping away from the dance to the rose arbor."

He arched a brow and gave a mock gasp. "You mean they had our number all along?"

"According to Bert, they weren't fooled for a minute."

He threw back his head and laughed. "And here we thought we were being so smooth."

"As I recall, you did have some pretty smooth moves."

He turned his head and studied her. "It's very satisfying to know you haven't forgotten."

Though she kept her smile in place, her tone softened. "I haven't forgotten any of it, Jase."

He closed a hand over hers, studying the ways their fingers reflexively linked. "Neither have I." He surprised her by lifting her hand to his mouth. "You could come up to my room. We could remember together."

She lifted startled eyes to his and saw him watching her with the wariness of a mountain cat.

"I don't think so." She pulled her hand away and got to her feet. "I'd better go."

"Don't." He stood and closed his hands over her upper arms. "Don't go, Em. Stay with me."

"Jason…" She closed her eyes and felt the brush of his mouth on hers. Just a brush, but it was enough to have her blood pulsing, her heart hammering.

Heat poured between them. When he took the kiss deeper she could feel herself sinking into him, inviting the flash and sizzle she knew would follow.

His arms came around her, holding her so firmly against him she could feel the pounding of his heart inside her own chest; the beat as erratic as her own.

His mouth was warm and firm and so tempting as it glided over hers. The hands at her back were setting off sparks. She struggled to ignore the sudden, hungry yearning. "I really have to go."

"You don't mean that."

"I do."

His breath came out in a huff of breath as he drew her close, pressing his chin to the top of her head while he steadied himself with his hands on her shoulders.

At last he drew in a ragged breath. "Come on. I'll walk you to your car."

They avoided the dining room, following instead the stone walkway that circled the Harbor House and led to the front porch.

Without a word she handed her ticket to the valet, who dashed off into the darkness to retrieve her car. She and Jason stood ramrod straight, without touching.

When the valet drove up, Jason settled her inside her car and leaned in the open window. He cupped her chin in his hand and looked into her eyes. "I don't like lying to myself."

"What's that supposed to mean?"

"I've been telling myself that I came back to honor an old teacher. And maybe I did. But I really came back to see you, Emily. I needed to settle some old issues."

"Are they settled?"

Instead of answering he brushed a quick kiss over her mouth, then straightened and turned away.

He saw the beam from her headlights as her car started forward along the curving drive. Tucking his hands in his pockets, he sprinted up the steps and stood watching from the porch until the lights faded from sight. Then he stepped into the foyer and headed toward the elevator.

As he pushed the button and waited for the door to close, he felt a shiver along his spine, as though someone watched.

The door creaked shut and the ancient elevator shuddered and lurched before depositing him on the third floor.

He was deep in thought as he let himself into his room.

Chapter 9

Jason tossed aside his suit jacket and tie and tugged on the buttons of his shirt before rolling it into a ball and heaving it angrily against the cushions of the overstuffed chair beside his bed.

A maid had already turned down the linens and had left a mint and one perfect rose on the pillow. The inviting scene mocked him.

He hadn't intended to make such a foolish admission to Emily. The words had just tumbled out. Once spoken, there was no way to recall them.

He prided himself on his use of words. After all, he earned his living by them. A damned fine living. But right now he'd give everything he had to replay those last few minutes together and take back that foolish admission.

What ever had possessed him to bare his soul? It wasn't his style. He'd spent a lifetime keeping himself to himself. His childhood had been a special kind of hell knowing that half the town knew about his father's drunken abuse. Whatever few secrets he'd managed to have, they weren't meant to be shared. And this was one of them.

So what if he had come back because of her? He'd had no business admitting it so late in the game.

He flopped down in the chair and kicked off his shoes. For a moment he leaned his head back and closed his eyes. Then he got to his feet and started toward his computer across the room. He wasn't in the mood to be creative, but that had never stopped him before. He would close his mind to reality and lose himself in fiction.

Halfway there he paused to stare out the window at the sweep of lawn and gardens below. Leaning a hip against the sill, he frowned. Such a deceptively pretty picture. The flowers all silvery with dew in the moonlight. Their fragrance more lush than French perfume. The air blowing through the screen so fresh and clean it almost hurt to breathe it in.

He'd forgotten how special early summer was in this place. Warm days gave way to cool nights, with gentle breezes blowing in off the lake. No need for air-conditioning until the dog days of August. And even then the heat was made tolerable by the promise of crisp autumn not far behind.

He would always think of Emily in the summer. And in some small corner of his mind he would probably always be that lonely kid who'd stumbled upon her in his secret cave, and had lost his heart in an instant.

He would never have had the courage to leave her without the ultimatum that had been given him. And yet it had been by leaving her, leaving this place, that he'd found himself. It sounded crazy, but there it was. He'd had to sever all ties, cut himself off and in the process cut out his heart, in order to become the man he was meant to be.

With a sigh he moved away from the window and settled himself at the desk in the corner of the room. If he couldn't sleep, at least he could write. Once he became absorbed in the work, nothing else would matter.

At the knock on the door he looked up in annoyance. At this time of night it could only be some drunk who'd got off the elevator on the wrong floor. He returned his attention to the computer, until the knock sounded again. Louder this time.

With a muttered oath he pushed away from the desk and started toward the door.

"Yeah? Who is it?"

"Jason?"

At the sound of Emily's voice, he threw the security lock and yanked the door open. Then he simply stared.

She looked hesitant, and more than a little breathless. "May I come in?"

He stepped back and she brushed past him. He continued staring at her until she turned. He managed to gather his scattered thoughts and close the door before leaning against it.

She gave a quick, nervous laugh. "I was almost home when I realized that wasn't where I wanted to be." She tried not to stare, but it was a jolt seeing him barefoot and naked to the waist. All that expanse of hair-roughened skin and rippling muscles had her breath hitching. She took a step toward him while her voice lowered to a sultry purr. "Where I wanted to be was here. With you."

She didn't know what she'd expected. Maybe that he'd scoop her up with a shout of gratitude and do away with the need for words. Instead he stood perfectly still, watching her with a wariness that had her wondering if this had all been a terrible mistake.

She swallowed and pondered what to do now.

Her move, she thought. The choice had been hers. Now it was her game. Her rules. She'd stand or fall by them. At least she was doing something. She'd worry later whether she'd made the right decision.

"You talked about issues between us." She saw his eyes narrow fractionally and knew she'd struck a nerve. "I've got issues, too, Jase. But right now, all I care about is the fact that you're here. I don't want to waste any more precious time. For now, for tonight, I want to be here, with you."

When he stayed where he was she took a hesitant step closer and touched a hand to his cheek. Just a touch, but it had her heart hammering. "I see I've managed to catch you by surprise. Were you getting ready for bed?"

"Working."

For the first time she noticed the computer on his desk quietly humming, the words on the screen a blur from this distance. "Oh, Jase. I'm sorry. I didn't mean to interrupt your work."

Before she could draw away, his fingers closed over her wrist, holding her still. "Work doesn't matter. You do."

That had her head coming up sharply. The simple press of his fingers on her flesh had her pulse leaping. "You're not annoyed?"

"Annoyed? Is that what you think?" His eyes burned into hers. "After all these years of wondering about you, wanting you, I'm just not sure I believe any of this."

"You wondered about me? Wanted me?" A tiny smile tugged at the corner of her mouth. "That's a relief. As for my being here, believe it, Jase."

He gave a quick shake of his head. "Better not smile yet. You might want to reconsider. I'm in a…mood. I'm not sure I can be gentle."

His admission had her breath coming out in a sigh of quiet relief. "If I wanted gentle, I'd snuggle one of my kittens."

That brought a quick laugh. "According to Trudy, there are enough of them." He looked down at the marks he'd left on her wrist. "I don't want to hurt you, Em."

"You already have. More than you know."

He absorbed the blow to his heart before dragging her close to press his mouth to a tangle of hair at her temple. "Then be warned. It can happen again. I can't make you any promises."

"I'm not asking for any." She lifted her face

until her lips found his. "I'm here because I want to be. Now kiss me quickly, before I lose my nerve."

"You?" His lips curved into a smile even as they skimmed her mouth. "You've always been absolutely fearless."

She took his hand and placed it between her breasts. "Then why is my poor heart pounding?"

"Is it? I thought that was mine." His smile faded as he studied the curve of her breasts, the uneven rise and fall of her chest with each breath.

He lifted his hands to frame her face. "You always had the power to make me lose control."

"I wish I'd known that."

"I hated admitting it, even to myself. But it was always there." The look in his eyes was intense. And then his mouth was on hers, moving ever so slowly to taste, to tease.

As the need grew, he deepened the kiss and began to feast.

She'd never forgotten these lips. Warm. Firm. And the taste of him. Dark, mysterious, smooth as brandy. It was so easy to let herself slip away. To remember another time when they'd been so young, so eager. But this wasn't like before. Now there was an edge of hunger, of passion, of hard, driving need that rose up, hot and sharp, catching her by surprise.

He knew the moment she lost herself in the kiss. Could feel the way her body softened, even while her hands tightened at his waist.

"I need to see you, Emily. All of you." His fingers were already busy with the zipper of her dress, sliding it from her shoulders in one quick motion, then watching as it pooled at her feet.

Her bra was nothing more than wispy bits of nude silk. Her hose were nude as well, and she wore nothing under them. He wasn't even aware that he sighed aloud at the sight of that slender body, those high, firm breasts and long, long legs.

"I didn't think it was possible, Emily, but you actually improved with age."

She laughed, though her throat felt dry as dust. "Gee, Jase. Just what a girl likes to hear, that she's getting older."

"And better."

"I might say the same for you." She ran her hands lightly up his back, feeling the ridge of muscle beneath her fingertips. "You've been working out."

"Running, mostly." He resisted the urge to devour her. "It takes the kinks out after hours at the computer." His eyes warmed with humor. "There are other kinks I'd rather be working out right now.'' He claimed her lips and kissed her until they were both breathless, while his hands moved over her, lighting fires wherever they touched.

He felt the need for her rise up and grab him by the throat. A need so fierce he had to fight to bank it. The thought of taking her here and now and ending this gnawing hunger, was almost more than he could deny. But he'd waited so long. Had thought of her so often. Now that she was here with him he would have his fill.

He nibbled her shoulder, moving aside the thin strap with his teeth. He ran his hands over the smooth silk, then tugged it aside and filled his palms with soft flesh. He absorbed the quick rush of heat as he lowered his head to touch, to taste.

He heard the way her breath caught and thrilled to it. This was how he'd wanted her. All that cool control swept aside and the rebel he'd once known returned to his arms. Where she belonged, he thought fiercely. Here with him. And to hell with the world beyond this door.

In the lamplight she looked like a princess. Regal. Controlled. Untouchable. But he could read the slight flicker of something in her eyes. Fear? The thought made him bolder. He had a sudden desire to see her lose all control. In one quick movement he had her backed against the door. He ran a fingertip under the edge of her hose and tore them off in his haste. He tossed them aside before finding her, hot and moist.

Emily was too stunned to do more than clutch at him as he brought her to the first amazing peak. He gave her no time to recover as he crushed her mouth with his and kissed her until they were both breathless, again and again, until their sighs turned into gasps of need.

Their breathing was ragged now, their mood frantic. Emily reached a hand to the button at his waist, desperate to touch him as he was touching her.

When his clothes joined hers in a heap at their feet, she thrilled to the press of his body to hers. But if she thought he would finally end this wild-fire that raged between them, she was mistaken.

"Do you know how long I've dreamed of you, Em? Of this?"

She touched a hand to his cheek. "It was the same for me, Jase."

His smile was quick and dangerous. "I doubt you ever had the dreams I had. You can't even imagine some of the things I've dreamed of doing with you." He ran hot, wet kisses down the smooth column of her throat. "To you."

"Show me."

He lifted his head to stare into her eyes. "That might not be wise."

"That never stopped you before." Her mouth curved in the slightest grin. "Do I have to dare you?"

His eyes narrowed. "You know I could never resist a dare." He dragged her close and covered her mouth in a savage kiss. The cool wall at her back offered no relief from the heat of his body pressed to hers. The hands moving over her were almost bruising in their intensity.

No one had ever touched her like this. One minute with such tenderness, she felt like weeping. The next, with such hunger, she could do nothing more than hold on as she was swept along in a torrent of passion that threatened to drown her.

When her legs would no longer support her, she clung to him. Sensing her need, he swept her into his arms and started across the room. Before he reached the bed he stopped to claim her lips once more.

That was his undoing. She wrapped her arms around his neck and returned his kisses with a fervor that matched his. The need rose up, hot and sharp, stealing his breath. He dropped to his knees and settled her on the rug. Lying over her he brought his mouth to one breast, then the other, nibbling, teasing, until she thought she would go mad with need. He moved down her body, taking her higher, higher, to the very edge of madness, holding release just out of reach.

This was how he'd wanted her. Pulse racing. Breathing labored. All trace of control gone. Her eyes focused on him with such intensity, it pierced his heart. If only for tonight, she was his. All his.

When at last he entered her she let out a deep sigh as she wrapped her arms around his neck, drawing him down, drawing him in deeper, until, mad with desire, she began to move with him, climb with him.

Lungs burning, they rolled across the floor, climbing higher, then higher still. As they reached the crest he buried his lips in her throat and soared. It was the most unbelievable journey to a universe neither of them had ever known before.

Chapter 10

"You all right?" Jason muttered the words against her throat.

Emily absorbed a series of aftershocks and found she couldn't speak, so she merely nodded.

"Sorry, I was rough." He started to scramble up, but she wrapped her arms around his neck and held him still.

She pressed her mouth to his cheek. "Not rough. Amazing."

He wondered at the way his heart reacted. With a jittery little dance. "You were pretty amazing yourself, Dr. Brennan." He settled himself beside her and drew her close, nuzzling his mouth to a tangle of hair at her temple.

"I'm sorry I disturbed your work."

"You definitely did that. But it was the nicest distraction I've ever had." He pressed light kisses across her face. "I'm still finding it hard to believe you're here."

She gave a little laugh. "That makes two of us. When I turned my car around, I got so nervous, wondering if you were already asleep, I almost talked myself into turning back. Then, when I knocked and you didn't answer right away, I was all set to go back to the elevator and beat a cowardly retreat."

"I did think about ignoring the knock. I'm glad now I didn't follow my first instinct." He smoothed the hair from her cheek and stared down into her eyes. "Will you stay the night?"

"If you want me to."

"If I want…?" He framed her face with his hands and lowered his mouth to hers. Against her lips he muttered, "Oh yeah. I want."

On a sigh he took the kiss deeper, sending heat spiraling through her. She wrapped her arms around his waist and gave herself up to the pleasure.

As he burned a trail of kisses across her throat

she caught her breath and managed to whisper, "Just one thing, Jase."

"Hmm?" He barely paused as he brought his mouth lower.

"I think your bed would be a whole lot more comfortable than this rug."

That had him lifting his head to study her. "You've gone all fancy on me now, haven't you, Dr. Brennan? There was a time, not so very long ago, that you wouldn't even complain about a sandy beach and no blanket."

They were both laughing as he scooped her up and carried her across the room to his bed.

Once there he stretched out beside her and gathered her close. Against her lips he whispered, "Ah, you were right. This is much better. Now, if you don't mind, I'd like to show you some of those fantasies I talked about."

"I don't mind one bit." Emily twined her arms around his neck, loving the feel of his hands on her, his mouth on hers.

With every touch, with every kiss, she slid deeper into the pleasure, and deeper into that sweet, sensual place reserved just for lovers.

In the midnight darkness Emily awoke to the sound of someone trying the door. There was the scrape of a key, the rattle of the doorknob, and then silence.

Slipping out of bed she listened at the door and was certain she heard someone breathing on the other side.

''Who's there?'' she called softly.

There was a quick shuffling of footsteps and then the sound of the slow, creaking descent of the elevator.

She listened for several more seconds before returning to bed.

''Where'd you go?'' Jason's voice, muttered against her throat, had heat racing along her spine.

''I thought I heard someone trying to come in.''

''Just somebody at the wrong door.''

''I suppose so.'' When he dragged her against the length of him, she shrugged aside the lingering wisps of fear that had awakened her from a dead sleep.

''As long as we're both awake…'' His hands began a lazy exploration. ''…we may as well put the time to good use.''

That had her laughing. ''I would have thought you'd had enough by now.''

''I'll never have enough of you, Em.'' It was true, he thought as his lips closed over her breast, turning her laughter to a gasp of surprise. If he'd thought to put an end to the hunger, he was only fooling himself. Each time they came together, the need for her was sharper, deeper than the time before.

He banked the fire that blazed, wanting to show her, with slow, deep kisses and soft, whispered sighs, the things he couldn't say.

As his mouth began to work its magic, Emily gave a low moan of pleasure before her mind went blank, and once again she lost herself in him.

"How did you survive when you left Devil's Cove?" Emily had propped the pillows against the headboard, and sat watching while Jason brewed coffee in a little window alcove.

Outside, the sky was streaked with the first faint blush of dawn light.

He turned and smiled at the sight of her, hair in wild disarray, wearing only his shirt to cover her nakedness. "I became an expert at doing odd jobs. You want a rancher? I'm your man. A groundskeeper? I can do that. Your dog groomed? I'm the best."

"Dog grooming? Really?"

"You bet. After a week, I had more customers than I could handle." He filled two cups and handed one to her before climbing into bed beside her.

"When did you find time to write?"

"Nights, mostly." He sipped. "At first I thought I'd keep a journal of my travels. After a while I realized that the characters I met were far more interesting than the places I'd seen. Everyone has a story. And some of them are pretty gripping."

"It's one thing to hear someone's story. It's another to turn it into a bestselling novel."

"Luck. Timing."

She couldn't help but marvel at his easy dismissal of his talent. It was so like him. She'd never known Jason to put his ego on display.

He studied her over the rim of his cup.

She flushed under his scrutiny. "What's wrong?"

"Nothing. I just don't know why you bothered to put on my shirt."

She arched a brow.

He set aside his cup, before taking hers from her hand and setting it beside his on the nightstand. "Didn't you know it would just make me all the more determined to take it off you?" With his eyes steady on hers he drew her close, sliding the shirt from her shoulders as he did.

What was it about his touch, his kiss, that could

bring this weakness to her limbs? She was a bright, sensible woman. But all Jason had to do was touch her and she could feel her mind begin to cloud, her body go all soft and fluid.

She put a hand to his chest to slow his advance. "We were going to get up early, remember? And get a fresh start on the day."

"And we are." He ran whispering kisses over her face before claiming her lips. "I can't think of a better way to start the day than this."

Outside the window birds were just beginning their chorus. A breeze, carrying the perfume of roses from the gardens below, rippled the curtains. Out in the harbor a boat's horn sounded. But the man and woman locked in an embrace were oblivious to everything except each other. The world beyond their room no longer mattered. All the wounds of the past, all the worries for their future, slipped away as well. For now, for this moment, they'd found their own private paradise.

"Come with me to The Willows, Jase." Emily stood in the small bathroom, wearing the terry-cloth robe provided by the Harbor House, blowing her hair dry after a shower. "Sunday brunch is always a treat, especially when my sisters can make it there."

He leaned a hip against the sill and stared out at the expanse of lawn already filled with families enjoying the flower gardens that surrounded the gazebo. "I don't want to intrude on a family tradition."

"You wouldn't be intruding." She set aside the hair dryer before disrobing and slipping into her dress.

Before she could ask for help Jason crossed the room and reached for the back zipper. Instead of closing it, he slid his hands inside and drew her against the length of him. Against the nape of her neck he muttered, "If you wouldn't mind skipping brunch with your family, I can think of something else to occupy our time on a lazy Sunday morning."

"I'll just bet you can." She absorbed the quick flash of heat before turning around to face him. "Come with me, Jase. You'll enjoy yourself. And you know my family would love to see you again."

"I'd love to see them, too. I've no doubt I'd enjoy their company." He drew her close and nibbled her lips. "Does Trudy still make that fabulous cinnamon coffee cake?"

"Uh-hmm." She twined her arms around his neck. "And fresh strawberries in mounds of real whipped cream. Not to mention a platter of fried chicken and the most amazing country omelette with mushrooms and cheese you've ever tasted.''

"You're making me hungry."

She laughed and pressed her mouth to his throat. "Have I mentioned Trudy's freshly ground café latte?"

His hands tightened at her back. "Be still my heart."

"You'll come with me?"

"I don't see that I have a choice." He held her a little away. "Do you think, before we leave, there's time for...?"

"Glutton." She slapped his arm.

"All you have to say is yes or no."

She couldn't keep the smile from curving the corners of her mouth. "Quiet. I'm trying to figure out how much time we have."

"That does it." He scooped her up and carried her to the bed. "I promise I won't even muss your hair."

"That's the last time I trust you." Emily ran a brush through the tangles and examined her makeup in the mirror.

Jason stepped up behind her and grinned at their twin reflections. "Can I help it if you turn into an animal in bed?'' He gave her a quick kiss on the cheek before picking up his watch. "We're late for brunch."

"Not if we hurry." She snatched up her purse and shoes and was halfway out the door when he caught up with her.

"Will we take your car or mine?"

Emily thought a minute. "Mine. I'll drive you back whenever you want to leave."

"Deal."

They walked arm-in-arm to the elevator and used the descent to indulge in one last kiss. As they came to a shuddering halt Emily stepped away.

Seeing it, Jason grinned. "You think you're going to fool anyone with that little charade? By now, everybody who works here knows that you've been up in my room all night."

She couldn't help laughing. "What was I thinking? For a minute there I almost forgot that I'm back in Devil's Cove. By noon there won't be anyone left in town that hasn't heard."

"So let's just give them something to talk about." He linked his fingers with hers as they stepped out on the main floor, nodding greetings to the desk clerk before stepping out into brilliant sunlight.

Within minutes the valet brought Emily's car and they were heading through town.

Jason stared out the side window. "I can't believe all the development that's going on."

"Mom's in the thick of it. Her business is thriving. She'll be only too happy to tell you all about it over brunch." Emily swung up the driveway and came to a sudden stop. She turned to Jason with a smile of satisfaction. "We made it with minutes to spare."

He looked over at her with a silly grin.

Seeing it, she arched a brow. "What now?"

"Nothing." He stared pointedly at her dress. "Not that they won't figure it out anyway. But a family as shrewd as yours is hardly going to overlook the fact that you're wearing the same dress you were wearing when you left last night."

"My dress!" Emily stared down at the sexy column of red silk, then burst into peals of laughter. "Hardly appropriate for Sunday brunch."

"Where are you going?" As Jason stepped out of the car she was already heading toward the rear of the house.

"Through the back," she called over her shoulder. "And then upstairs to change. Cover for me."

"Sure. No problem." Laughing, he followed the sound of voices coming from the patio.

Chapter 11

"Jason." Bert looked up from the table and crossed the patio. "What a lovely surprise."

Jason bent to kiss his old teacher's cheek. "I hope I'm not intruding. Emily asked me to come to brunch."

"You're part of our family here, Jason. You know you're always welcome." Bert glanced around. "Where is Emily?"

"Up in her room. She'll be down in a few minutes."

"Good. I have you to myself, at least for a few minutes." The older woman linked her arm through his. "Trudy, look who's joining us for brunch."

The housekeeper beamed her approval before pouring a foaming glass of fresh orange juice and handing it to him. "The judge and Hannah are over in the gardens. I'm sure," she added dryly, "they're having a lively discussion about fertilizers and bug killers."

"Ladybugs," Courtney corrected. "Hannah is convinced they're the most efficient bug killer on the planet." She grinned at Jason as she smoothed the tablecloth and anchored it with an antique cachepot filled with bright yellow daisies.

Charley and Sidney looked up from the blueprints they'd been examining to call out greetings to Jason. As he ambled closer Charley explained, "The new development. Want to take a look?"

While Jason looked over her shoulder, Bert wrinkled her nose. "I can't tell anything from a blueprint. I need to see the finished product."

"It's easy enough, Bert. Here's the clubhouse." Charley traced a finger. "And over here are the townhouses. These are plots of land for homes, and this…" She drew a finger around the perimeter. "…will be a championship golf course. Up here in the hills they're planning equestrian trails, and stables for several dozen horses."

That had Bert chuckling. "Far enough away from the country club, I hope, to keep the ripe scent of horse manure from offending anyone."

"Horse manure." That had Hannah hurrying over, with her grandfather close behind her. "I've already put in a bid to handle the removal."

Courtney giggled. "Oh, be still my heart."

Hannah tossed her head. "You won't be making fun of it when you see what it does for your gardens."

"But will I be able to stand the smell of them?"

Before the teasing could erupt into a war, Sidney caught sight of Emily hurrying toward them, dressed in pale linen slacks and a matching top.

"A much better choice than the wrinkled red silk you were wearing when you got here."

"You were still in…?" Hannah gaped as the realization dawned.

Seeing the flush on her granddaughter's cheeks, Bert managed to deflect attention. "I believe Trudy is signaling us to take our places." She walked over to her husband and slipped her hand into his, before leading the way to the table.

Before following, Courtney leaned close to whisper, "It seems that some things never change, big sister."

When she ambled away, Emily glanced up at Jason's eyes.

She'd expected humor, and it was there. But there was something else, as well. A smoldering heat that had her heart tripping over itself as he rested a hand possessively on her shoulder. She and Jason took their seats beside the others at the big patio table.

"What's this?" The judge peered at the contents of the platter Trudy was holding.

"Whitefish." With Trudy's tobacco-roughened voice, it sounded more like a wheeze than a word.

"What happened to the fried chicken you usually make?"

"Miss Bert thought fish would be healthier." She speared a large portion and set it on his plate. "Try it, Judge."

Frank Brennan glanced across the table at his wife, who sat sipping her coffee. "Tell me, Bert, why you would ruin a perfectly good Sunday brunch with health foods."

"They're not health foods. They're just healthy."

"There's a difference?"

She merely smiled and helped herself to some of the fish while her husband took a larger than usual portion of omelette.

Charley glanced across the table at Jason, seated beside her oldest daughter. "Everywhere I look in town, I see someone reading your book."

"My kind of people," he said with a smile.

"I've had several clients express some hesitation about living in a town where a potential serial killer might be lurking. I've reassured them that you write fiction." She paused a beat before saying, "It is fiction, isn't it?"

He took his time setting down his cup. "It is. But there's no denying that it was suggested by what happened in Devil's Cove years ago."

Hannah looked on with interest. "I remember hearing about those murders. Weren't they found to be unrelated?"

Jason turned to the man seated at the head of the table. "The one to ask would be your grandfather. He was the presiding judge in one of the trials."

Frank Brennan nodded. "I remember it well. It was the first murder trial in my career, and stirred up quite a bit of interest, though I doubt if anyone outside our town gave a hoot about it. A teenage girl was found dead in a field. Strangled with her own shirt. A transient field hand was found sleeping off a drunk nearby. A jury found him guilty."

"What about the others?"

The old man shrugged. "Unrelated, as I recall. A young girl's body was found behind the sugar beet refinery. A guard at the refinery heard a scuffle, went out to investigate, and found the girl dead and saw a man running from the scene. He shot and killed him. Turned out to be a migrant worker, and an investigation exonerated the guard of any guilt."

"The third?" Intrigued, his granddaughter set down her fork, her food forgotten for the moment.

The judge shrugged. "An older teen who'd been drinking, apparently. Her body was found floating in the water just offshore. The sheriff figured she'd been skinny-dipping and become disoriented in the dark. It was considered an unfortunate drowning accident, the result of too much alcohol and too little sense." He turned to Jason. "How did you know I'd presided over the first trial?"

"I read the transcript, as well as the sheriff's reports and newspaper accounts."

"You do your own research, do you?"

Jason nodded.

"I'm impressed." The judge helped himself to a piece of fish, causing his wife to lift a brow in surprise. "I always figured you writers hired someone to do that for you."

"Some do, I suppose." Jason bit into the omelette and grinned at the housekeeper. "You haven't lost your touch, Trudy. This is amazing."

The older woman couldn't hide her pleasure as she began cutting cinnamon coffee cake into slices. When she passed them around, she put the biggest slice on Jason's plate. That had Emily and her sisters exchanging knowing smiles. Their housekeeper's fondness for this man hadn't been diminished by the passage of so many years.

The family lingered over coffee, watching the parade of boats on the water, and speculating on the changes their town would experience with the newest development.

The judge sighed. "Devil's Cove won't be a small town much longer."

"True." His wife set aside her empty cup. "And a bigger town means bigger problems."

Emily looked over at her grandmother. "Is that why you decided to give up teaching?"

"Not at all." Bert shook her head. "It was just time to step aside and make room for a younger teacher. But I haven't given it up completely. I've already told the board I'll be available to tutor any students who need individual attention."

She saw Jason studying her and gave him a gentle smile. "Who knows? Maybe the next troubled boy or girl will turn out to be my senator one day."

Her husband held her chair and offered his arm as she got to her feet. With a wink he asked, "Why not go for a president?"

"Why not, indeed?" She gave him a quick kiss on the cheek. "After all, there was a time when I set my sights on the smartest, best-looking young lawyer in town and got him."

"And I say thank heavens for it." He turned to the others at the table. "I'm taking my bride for a walk, to work off all this fine food. Any takers?"

One by one the others pushed away from the table.

Charley touched a napkin to her mouth and got to her feet. "Sorry. I'm needed at my office."

"On Sunday?"

"The developer is flying in a team of architects. I promised to meet with them."

"I have a landscaping job that won't wait until tomorrow." Hannah kissed her grandmother's cheek.

Courtney followed suit. "I'm needed at my shop. With so many in town for Bert's tribute, it'll be mobbed."

Sidney glanced at the sun, now high overhead. "I have to get back to my painting while the light is still good."

The judge paused to consider his last remaining

granddaughter. "Emily? Would you and Jason like to join us, or do the two of you have other plans as well?"

Before Emily could respond, Bert caught her husband's hand and turned him away. "If you don't mind, I'd like you all to myself. And I suspect those two young people feel the same way."

With a laugh they started across the lawn, leaving Emily and Jason alone on the patio.

"Alone at last." Jason leaned close, then looked up to see Trudy just heading toward them. With a muttered oath he stepped back. "Looks like I spoke too soon. How do you manage to get any privacy in a crowd like this?"

Emily caught his hand. "Come on. I know just the place."

She led him across the patio and around to the rear of the house. As soon as they were out of sight of the housekeeper, Jason drew her into his arms and covered her mouth with his.

Emily felt the quick rush of heat and thrilled to it. As he took the kiss deeper she wrapped her arms around his neck.

Against his mouth she whispered, "Why don't we take this inside, away from any possible intrusions."

"I like the way you think, Doctor Brennan."

With a laugh she reached into her pocket and withdrew a ring of keys. "I keep my clinic closed on Sunday, except for emergencies."

As she turned, Jason nibbled the back of her neck. "This is definitely an emergency."

They were laughing as she bent to insert a key. Before she could, the door slid open.

Her laughter died in her throat.

She stared at the open door for a moment in silence before turning to Jason. "Someone's been in here."

"Are you sure?" He saw the alarm in her eyes. "Maybe Melissa forgot to lock it last night."

"Mel left before me. I locked up last night. And I distinctly recall locking this door."

"Your family?"

She shook her head. "They don't have keys. Besides, they would never come around to the rear door. If they'd wanted to gain access, they'd have come in through the house entrance."

"Stay here." He stepped inside and walked from room to room, opening doors to the examining rooms, checking closets for places to hide. When he was content that no one was hiding inside, he returned to the door and held it for Emily.

"Maybe you'd better check out any drugs you keep here."

Without a word she went to the locked cabinet. Finding it undisturbed, she walked from room to room, looking for anything that might be out of place.

Jason nodded toward the file cabinet. "Would someone want to go through your files?"

She shrugged. "For what reason? Except for a list of medical conditions, I can't think of any use they'd be to an intruder." Still, she opened each drawer, checking to see if any file folders appeared to be in disarray.

She returned to the reception area and began to pace. "Why would someone go to the trouble of breaking in, and then leave without taking anything?"

He shook his head. "I don't know. Are you absolutely certain you locked that door?"

She shrugged. "I thought so. Now I'm not so sure."

Seeing the way she held herself stiffly, arms wrapped across her chest, he locked the door and crossed to her side.

She appeared startled. "What are you doing?"

Without a word he gathered her close, pressing his mouth to a tangle of hair at her temple.

"Jason? What are you...?"

He scooped her up and started into one of the

examining rooms. Once inside he kicked the door shut and lowered his mouth to hers.

Against her lips he murmured, "I've always found the best way to ponder a mystery is by doing something to divert my attention."

"I see. Is that all I am? A diversion?"

"The best." He cut off the protest she was about to make, kissing her, long and slow and deep, until heat rose up, pulsing between them.

When at last she came up for air she managed to mumble, "Umm. I suppose you mean that as a compliment."

"You bet. And since we've finally escaped that big, noisy family of yours, I figure there's no sense letting this precious privacy go to waste."

She gave a laugh of pure delight. "I'm beginning to like the way you think."

He ran hot, nibbling kisses down her throat. "I figured you would."

Chapter 12

Emily jogged down the curving driveway of The Willows and hit the main street at a run. Because of the dense fog rolling in off the lake, the street-lights were little more than golden halos, visible only when she was directly beneath them. At this time of the morning hardly anyone in Devil's Cove was up.

When she'd been at University Hospital, she'd had the use of one of the finest cardiovascular workout centers, with state-of-the-art equipment. Now she jogged to the local YMCA and did a quick round on their machines before following up with laps in the pool. What had begun as an inconvenience was now a source of real pleasure to her. She found that she liked having the streets of the town to herself. Loved watching the changing scene, from spring to summer, from a hot, muggy morning to one like this, with fingers of fog chilling her heated flesh.

"'Morning, Doc." Albert, the high-school custodian, performed the same service at the Y during his summer break. He barely looked up from the magazine he was reading.

"Good morning, Albert." It occurred to Emily that this building smelled the same as her old high school. That indefinable smell of locker rooms, pool chemicals and disinfectant.

She stepped into the workout room and noted that several regulars were already there.

"Hi, Emily." Ted Johnson, the bank manager, lean and trim at fifty, was busy at the rowing machine.

Emily waved as she approached the stair-stepper.

"Hey, Dr. Brennan." Bret Drummond was a high-school senior who worked for Emily's sister, Hannah, during the summer to stay in shape for football season.

"Hey, yourself. Have you decided that laying

sod and digging trenches isn't enough exercise, Bret?''

''I figured I'd push a little harder.'' With a grin he returned his attention to the weights.

Across the room Emily saw Chief Boyd Thompson working up a sweat on one of the treadmills. He didn't bother to acknowledge her as he continued on at a steady pace.

Emily went through her routine, moving easily from the stair-stepper to the rowing machine vacated by Ted Johnson, and finally to weights.

Much later, satisfied with her workout, she stepped into a dressing room and stripped down to her bathing suit before placing her keys in her shoe and stashing everything in a locker.

The best part of her workout was swimming laps. Growing up in Devil's Cove, she'd been swimming since she was old enough to walk. She'd always loved the water. There was solace in the simple act of diving in and feeling herself enclosed in a warm cocoon. Now, as she swam the length of the pool, then back, she allowed herself to think about the one thing she'd been avoiding.

This time she'd spent with Jason had been a revelation. It was as if the years had melted away, and they'd never been apart. All the old feelings were still there. They could talk for hours without run-

ning out of things to say. They could go for long
stretches of time without speaking and feel none
of the awkwardness that usually cropped up between two people. It was as though they were completely in sync. Hearts, minds, souls. With Jason
she had discovered something else that had been
missing from her life as well. Passion. From that
first frantic tug at her heart, to the pulse-pounding
need whenever he touched her, there was no denying the effect he had on her. His kisses packed
a punch that no drug could ever duplicate. It ought
to be thrilling, and it was. But it was also terrifying.

   She was frowning as she pulled herself from the
pool and started toward the lockers. Was that why
she'd insisted on returning to her own place last
night, even though the temptation to stay the night
with him had been almost overwhelming? Hadn't
she fooled herself into believing that she could
simply enjoy being with Jason for a week, and then
get on with her life as it had been before? Now
she was beginning to realize that, though she
thought of herself as older and wiser, the truth was,
she couldn't avoid being hurt. Oh, she'd be able to
put a good face on it. But when he left, it would
be every bit as painful as before.

   Glancing around she realized the others were al-

ready gone. She turned the combination lock and
was reaching for her clothes when she suddenly
froze.

She'd put her keys in her shoe, and set her jogging clothes on top. Now they were in disarray,
with her clothing tossed carelessly to one side, and
her shoes turned over. After a few frantic seconds
she located her keys lying under the pile of clothes.

She stood a moment, puzzling over this. It was
clear to her that the one responsible for rifling
though her things had made no effort to hide it.
But why? To annoy her? To frighten her? To warn
her that she was vulnerable?

If so, it had had the desired effect. Heart pounding, she took a deep breath and closed herself in a
dressing cubicle. When she stepped out minutes
later, she hurried outside and set a brisk pace for
the run home. Once there she showered and
dressed for a day at the clinic, grateful that her
busy schedule would keep her mind off this latest
mystery.

Melissa poked her head in the examining room.
''That's the last patient of the day.''

''Thanks, Mel.'' Emily made some final notes
in the file before handing the folder over to her
assistant. ''Are you going to the play tonight?''

Melissa nodded. "Wouldn't miss it. I think the entire town will be there." As she stepped into the reception area she called, "Hi, Jason. The doctor is in, but only if you're not here as a patient."

"You can count on that."

Emily looked up as he filled the doorway. A moment later he closed the door and leaned against it before dragging her into his arms.

Against her lips he whispered fiercely, "You should have stayed the night."

She absorbed the familiar rush of heat and clung to him a moment, loving the feel of his mouth, rough and possessive, on hers. "I needed…" She put a hand to his chest and sucked in a quick, shuddering breath. "…to get back to my routine."

"God knows I don't want to get in the way of that, Em. But I spent a miserable night wishing you were with me."

She gave a shaky laugh. "Yeah. Me, too."

"Good. It's nice to know I'm not alone in this madness."

From the other side of the door came Melissa's muffled voice. "Good night, you two. See you at the play."

Before Emily could reply she was dragged close for another kiss. This time she gave herself up to it completely, loving the feel of Jason's arms holding her close while his mouth plundered hers.

When at last he lifted his head, the fire in his eyes had her heart hitching. "I know I promised you dinner before the play, Em. But I'm afraid if I don't soon get some time alone with you, I'll devour you."

Without a word she took his hand and led him out of the clinic and up the back stairs to her room. Once inside she closed the door and turned to him.

He drew her into his arms. "You don't mind? If you do…"

She touched a finger to his mouth. With a smile she whispered, "We can have dinner anytime, Jase. Right now I want the same thing you want."

And then there was no need for words as they took each other with all the fury of a summer storm.

Emily picked up a shawl and was about to open the door to her room when Jason's arms came around her and he drew her back against the length of him.

"You're sure you've named everyone who was at the Y this morning?"

"I'm sure." She paused before adding, "Jase, nothing was taken."

"That's just it. Nothing was taken from your clinic, either. But someone is working overtime to get your attention. We need to figure out why."

"Maybe it's just someone's idea of a prank."

He turned her to face him. "Has this ever happened before?"

She shook her head.

"Then maybe it isn't just being done for your sake."

"What's that supposed to mean?"

He shrugged. "There are no secrets in Devil's Cove. By now everyone knows that you're spending time with me. Let's not forget that there are plenty of people in this town who resent me for the book I wrote."

"You said it was fiction."

"Based on something that actually happened here in Devil's Cove. And from my research, I drew conclusions. Fictional ones, but conclusions all the same."

"Are you saying that there really could be a murderer here in our town who is afraid of what you know?"

"I wish I had the answer to that." He met her eyes. His own were narrowed in thought. "I never wanted to put you in harm's way, Emily. I want you to promise me that you'll be careful."

She was already shaking her head. "If you think I'm going to give up jogging, working out, putting in evenings in my clinic…"

"I wouldn't even suggest such a thing. Just don't take any chances. You can do those things without being careless."

When she started to draw away he tightened his grasp on her upper arms. "Promise me."

She gave a sigh before nodding. "I'll be careful."

"Good girl."

He led the way down the stairs and out the door to his car. When they were settled he gave her a smile. "I like the title of the play. *An Orchid for Mrs. B.* Let's see if the high-school drama club is any better than we were."

Though he managed to keep his smile in place, he found himself glancing around as they parked and made their way through the crowded assembly in the high-school auditorium to their assigned seats with the rest of Emily's family.

As the lights went down and he struggled to follow the plot of the lighthearted play, Jason had the prickly feeling that someone nearby was watching. Throughout the play he couldn't shake the feeling.

Chapter 13

"What did you think, Mrs. B?" One of the student actors addressed Bert, who was basking in the afterglow.

"Would you prefer a critique of the writing or the acting?" She stood, arms laden with orchids, which had been presented on-stage by a cast member, to thunderous applause from the audience. Now, as the crowd began to drift away, she remained with the actors and their families, enjoying the moment.

Without waiting for a reply she went on. "I found the writing to be first-rate. You make this old English teacher very proud. As for the acting,

I won't be at all surprised to see some of you on Broadway in a few years.''

That had the students beaming with pride.

''Were you surprised?'' one of the girls asked.

''Not at all. I've always known that Devil's Cove was blessed with an abundance of talented young people.'' She turned to Bret Drummond. ''But I had no idea that behind those muscles you harbored such comic genius.''

While the others slapped his arm and gave him high-fives, Bret's cheeks turned bright red. ''I didn't know it either, Mrs. B. But once I got into the script, it was really easy.''

''Football's loss may be Hollywood's gain,'' Bert said with a smile. ''Now. I understand the cast is heading over to the Daisy Diner to celebrate. Do you mind if the Brennan family joins you?''

The students couldn't hide their delight. While some of them ducked backstage to remove their makeup, the others led the way out of the auditorium and down the street to the diner, with Bert and her husband in the midst of them.

Trailing behind were Jason and Emily and her sisters, as well as Robeson Ryder and Prentice Osborn.

As soon as they exited the school, Jason was able to put aside his concerns. Or maybe it was simply that he was as caught up in the festive mood as the others. The closer they got to the diner, the more Emily could feel him beginning to relax.

She turned to Robeson. "I hope Carrie is working tonight so she can share some of this fun."

Robeson nodded. "She'll be there. I asked her to join us at the play, but she said she was scheduled for a double shift."

Prentice jammed his hands in his pockets. "She works too hard."

"I don't see that she has much choice." Robeson fell into step beside him. "It has to be tough raising a daughter alone."

"If I had my way she wouldn't be alone." The minute the words were out of his mouth, Prentice looked uncomfortable.

The others simply stared.

It was Robeson who finally broke the silence. "You…and Carrie?"

Prentice stared hard at the toe of his Italian leather loafer, which had likely cost more than Carrie could earn in a week. "Only in my mind. Apparently she's carrying a torch for someone else."

Jason gave him a steady look. "Have you asked?"

Prentice shrugged, clearly feeling embarrassed

to be having this discussion. "I've asked her out a few times, but she always has an excuse."

"Maybe she just thinks you're out of her league." Robeson paused beside him. "After all, her mother cleans your house."

"What's that got to do with anything?" Prentice moved along with the others.

"Well, you do have to admit that it would feel a little strange to date your mother's boss."

Prentice shrugged. "I don't think Carrie would even think of such a thing. I know I don't. She's the kindest person I've ever known. You ought to see the way she takes care of my brother Will. The minute he walks into the diner, she starts his grilled cheese sandwich, with the crusts cut off just the way he likes it, and a thick vanilla milkshake."

Robeson nodded. "She's always had a good heart."

"She's a good mother to Jenny, too."

Jason grinned. "Have you ever bothered to tell Carrie what you're telling us?"

Again that almost shy shrug that seemed so out of character in the man who most in the town would have described as smug and self-satisfied. A man accustomed to having everything he'd ever wanted.

As they stepped inside the diner they were assaulted by the scent of onions on the grill, and an almost manic level of noise from the throng that had already gathered. In the middle of it all, Carrie was like a whirlwind of work and easy laughter and chatter as she catered to the mixed crowd of teens and their families.

After moving several tables together, the Brennans and their guests found themselves in the very center of the crowd.

Almost at once Carrie was there to take their orders.

"Mrs. B." She leaned close to give the older woman a hug. "I'm sorry I missed the play. Was it as good as I've heard?"

"Even better, Carrie." Bert returned the hug. "I think it's safe to say we'll have coffees and burgers all around, with lots of those cheesy fries that have become your specialty."

"I didn't know you were an expert on the Daisy Diner's menu," Carrie said with a laugh.

"Oh, I've heard enough to know it's one of the town's best-kept secrets." Bert glanced around. "Does anyone want anything different?"

When the others shook their heads, Carrie tucked away her pad and pencil and was soon passing out steaming cups of coffee.

As Carrie moved among the crowded tables Jason leaned close to Prentice. "Why didn't Will come to the play?"

"He wanted to stay home. Carrie's mom gives me a hand with him, and tonight she had Carrie's daughter with her. Will adores Jenny. Whenever she's there, you can't pry Will away."

Jason couldn't help teasing his old friend. "Careful. The way you're watching Carrie, someone might get the same idea about you and Jenny's mom."

Prentice flushed and managed to look away. "Am I that obvious?"

Jason decided to let him off the hook. "So, what do Will and Jenny do together?"

"She's teaching him to play checkers. Nobody else could ever get him to sit still long enough to learn. She has such patience with him."

"So do you, Prentice. You're a good brother."

"I try. Sometimes it isn't easy. But I promised my folks I'd always be there for Will."

Overhearing, Robeson leaned across the table to say, "I know something both Will and Jenny would enjoy. And it would give you the perfect excuse to ask Carrie to come along." Seeing his friend's arched brow he said with a smile, "The fireworks."

Prentice seemed to mull that over as Carrie

moved around the tables serving their late-night meal and topping off their coffees.

When he glanced at Emily for confirmation she nodded her head. "Why not? You have nothing to lose, Prentice."

"And maybe, if you're lucky," Jason said under his breath, "you'll get everything you've ever wanted." He saw Emily's eyes soften, and knew he'd touched a nerve. Under the cover of the tablecloth his hand found hers and squeezed.

When he looked up, he saw the way Bert was watching them. She merely smiled, and he couldn't contain the laughter that bubbled up.

"What's so funny?" Emily glanced over.

"Your grandmother. She's the slyest woman I've ever known."

Robeson nodded. "I always swore Mrs. B. had eyes in the back of her head."

"And the sharpest mind around." Jason turned to Prentice. "If you really want to know who your rival is, all you have to do is ask your old teacher. She knows everything about everyone in Devil's Cove."

Prentice chuckled. But they could see the wheels turning in his head. There was no doubt that Mrs. Brennan was the keeper of all her students' secrets. If Carrie actually was in love with someone else, her old teacher would know about it. Whether she would be willing to share that secret was another question.

When the others finally got up to leave, Prentice decided he wanted one last cup of coffee.

As he ambled over to the counter and took a seat, Jason winked at Emily. "I'm tempted to tease him and say we'll wait with him."

"Why don't you?"

He caught her hand and led her toward the door. Leaning close he whispered, "Because I'm afraid he'll take me up on my offer. And at the moment all I can think about is getting you alone."

She turned. "My place or yours?"

"Mine. It's closer."

She laid a hand on his. "Good plan."

They trailed the others who were headed toward the high-school parking lot where they'd left their cars. Once again fog had begun rolling in, blurring the lights of the town, muting the sounds of boats in the harbor.

Jason breathed deeply. "No matter where I've traveled in the world, the smell of a harbor always carries me back to Devil's Cove. I'll never be able to see fog without thinking of home."

"I'm the same way." Emily draped an arm around his waist, loving the feel of his arm around her shoulders. She snuggled close. "You seemed distracted during the play. Is something wrong?"

He shrugged. "The whole time we were in the auditorium I had the feeling that I was being watched."

She stopped in her tracks. "You, too?"

He looked at her. "You felt it?"

She nodded. "I tried to shake it off, but I wasn't really comfortable until we were at the diner."

He nodded. "Exactly." He drew her close and they continued walking until they reached his car. "So, are we both being paranoid, or is something sinister going on here?"

"I don't know, Jase." Emily settled herself beside him.

They drove in silence until they reached the Harbor House.

She followed him into the hotel, and they stepped into the elevator, which began its creaky ascent. "Without some sort of proof, all we have are feelings."

"We have much more than that." When the elevator opened he led her to his door and fumbled for his key. "There's the break-in at your clinic. The incident in your locker. And we both…" Before he could insert the key the door moved inward.

He motioned for Emily to wait outside while he walked in and snapped on the lights. After checking the closet and bathroom, and finding both empty, he caught her hand and brought her inside, locking the door behind her.

She glanced at the computer humming on his desk. "Did you leave that on?"

"No." He stepped closer and began a quick check of his programs. "Nothing's been disturbed. Probably because it requires a password to open my files."

Emily glanced around uneasily. "Did you leave anything of value in the room?"

"Nothing." He walked to the window and looked out at the expanse of lawn and gardens, gilded by moonlight. "Whoever wants to get our attention has succeeded."

"Are you going to call down to the desk and report the break-in?"

He shook his head and crossed to her, drawing her into his arms. "It would just be one more distraction." The look in his eyes was pure danger, sending her heart into a tailspin. He lowered his head and poured all his feelings into a kiss that had her head spinning, her breath backing up in her throat. "And right now, Emily, you're the only distraction I want."

* * *

Emily awoke to the creak of the elevator. Moments later she heard the slight rattle of the doorknob, and knew that someone was standing outside the room.

"Jase." Her voice was little more than a whisper, her hand on his arm the briefest of touches, but he was awake at once.

He sat up and without a word started across the room. At the same moment they heard retreating footsteps, and the sound of the elevator descending.

Jason picked up the phone and rang the desk. Because of the late hour it rang several times before it was answered.

"Yes, Mr. Cooper?" The young woman's voice sounded sleep-roughened.

"Would you see who gets off the elevator, please?"

"The elevator? Just a moment." A few minutes later the voice was back, sounding much more alert. "I'm sorry, sir. The elevator is here on the main floor, but it's empty."

"Do you have a security camera in the elevator?"

"We do, sir."

"Would you check with your manager and see

if I might be allowed to view the security tape tomorrow?''

''Yes, sir. Is there anything else?''

''No. Thank you.'' He hung up the phone and returned to bed, drawing Emily close.

Against his mouth she whispered, ''I'm worried, Jase. Why would someone do this?''

''Hard to say. To a twisted mind, it might be just a game.''

''But someone's going to a lot of trouble.''

''Yeah. That's what I'm thinking, too. This sort of thing has a way of turning deadly.''

He felt her shiver and hated the fact that his words had added to her fears. Lowering his mouth to her temple, he began to brush soft, whispery kisses over her upturned face. ''I don't think you have anything to worry about tonight. My door is locked. The front desk has been alerted. And even our merry prankster has to sleep sometime.''

He heard her sigh as she wrapped herself around him. For now, for this brief time, he would ease her worries the only way he could.

Chapter 14

"Look at that sunshine." Dressed in Jason's shirt, Emily was standing at the window of his hotel room, sipping coffee.

"I'd rather look at you." He walked up behind her and drew her close.

She shivered as his hands brushed the underside of her breasts. Even that simple touch had heat pouring through her.

"It's going to be perfect weather for the last day of Bert's tribute."

"The last day." Jason shook his head. "I can't believe I've been here a week." He lowered his head to nuzzle her neck. "From the minute I drove into town, it was as though I'd never been gone."

"I felt that way when Dad got sick and I came home to help. I was sure I'd miss the excitement of the University Hospital. The morning rounds. The eager students. The comfort level of having other doctors around to assist whenever there was a crisis."

Jason's hands stilled. He stepped aside to pour himself a cup of coffee. "Your grandmother mentioned one doctor in particular."

"David?" That had Emily turning to him with an arched brow. "Now why would she mention him?"

"Knowing Mrs. B, it was probably calculated to see my reaction."

"Ah." Emily sipped before asking, "And just what was your reaction?"

"I was jealous as hell."

She couldn't help grinning. "You were?"

"Don't look so smug, Dr. Brennan."

"It's just nice to know that I caused you a moment's concern."

"More than a moment." He leaned against the windowsill and regarded her over the rim of his cup. "In all the years I've been gone, you were never far from my mind, Emily."

"Is that why you never bothered to write or call me?"

He frowned into his cup. "I had my reasons."

They both looked over when the phone rang. Jason swore at the timing before picking it up. "Jason Cooper." He paused, listened, before saying, "I'll meet him in your office in an hour."

He replaced the receiver and turned to Emily. "The hotel security officer is on his way. He has to be present before I can be allowed to view the tape. I'd like you to come along. When we've finished, I'll take you to breakfast. There's something I need to tell you."

Emily shook her head. "I have to get to the clinic. My first appointment is in at nine."

"I'm sorry, Em." He crossed the room and drew her close. Against her temple he muttered, "Can we get together before dinner?"

"We can try. I asked Mel to schedule my last appointment no later than three, so that I'd have time to get ready for tonight."

"I'll come by the clinic then."

She nodded and started toward the shower, then paused when she realized Jason was following.

At her questioning look he merely smiled. "I just thought we could save time by showering together."

"Uh-huh. You know where that always leads."
But she offered no protest as she stripped off his
shirt and stepped under the warm spray with him.

Mel opened the door to the examining room.
"That's it. No more patients. Let's get out of here
before somebody shows up on the doorstep."

With a laugh Emily nodded. "Good idea, Mel.
Did Jason call?"

"Twice. Once when you were with Mrs. Mon-
roe. The other time when you were examining the
Halleran baby. He said he'd try again later."

Emily brushed aside the twinge of frustration.
There simply weren't enough hours in the day. Especially a busy day like this. "Okay. I'll see you
in a couple of hours."

She finished her notes and closed the file folder
with a sigh. She'd skipped lunch and worked non-
stop through the day, hoping for some time to relax
before facing the crowd expected for the banquet
and fireworks that would officially close the festivities for her grandmother.

She had thought the week-long activities would
be a drain on Bert, but instead the old woman
seemed energized by the return of so many of her
former pupils. She had filled almost every hour of
the past week meeting with them, getting to know

their spouses and families, collecting addresses and phone numbers so that she could keep in touch in the years to come. If anything, she seemed to be walking with more spring in her step each day.

Emily set aside the file and pressed a hand to the small of her back before heading toward the outer office. Maybe she was the one getting older. This week was beginning to take its toll on her, both physically and emotionally.

She stopped in midstride when she realized she wasn't alone.

Albert Sneed stood by her desk, his hand wrapped in a bloody towel.

"That's a lot of blood, Albert. What happened?"

He frowned. "Got careless. Was fixing a treadmill over at the Y and it almost chewed off a finger."

"Why don't you go in the examining room and I'll take a look. If it's too serious, I may have to send you to the University Hospital."

He paused to glance at the clock over her desk. "I'd rather you'd deal with it here, but I suppose you'll be wanting to get ready for the big shindig in town."

"That's all right, Albert. I always have time for an emergency. Now let's take a look at that hand."

He stood aside and waited until she'd stepped inside before pulling the door closed.

Seeing it she smiled. "There's no need to close the door, Albert. With Mel gone, I'll probably have to fetch sutures, not to mention an antibiotic, before we're through."

"I wouldn't count on it. You see, I waited until I was sure your assistant was gone before coming in." To her surprise he tossed aside the bloody towel. "Red dye. I thought we could have a lot more fun alone."

Emily's stomach clenched when she saw the glint of steel, revealing what he'd kept hidden beneath the towel. In his hand was a very shiny, very sharp knife.

Jason glanced at his watch as he waited for the valet to bring his car. He'd been tied up all day, first with the head of security for the hotel, and then with Chief Boyd Thompson. It had taken all Jason's powers of persuasion to get Boyd to abandon his paperwork to swing by the Harbor House and view the security tape. Even after seeing it, the chief had been reluctant to believe Albert Sneed's presence in the hotel elevator could signal any sort of danger.

"He's assisted in maintenance here for years.

The manager said it isn't at all unusual for him to check out the elevator at odd hours, when he's through with his work at the Y, or over at the schoolhouse. That old guy's been around Devil's Cove since the Stone Age. What right do you have coming back here and throwing your celebrity around to make him out to be some kind of evil villain?"

"This wasn't my choice, Boyd. I didn't invite him up for fun and games. Ever since I got here he's been stalking me."

"So you say."

"And stalking Emily. Her clinic was broken into."

At that Boyd's head came up sharply. "Why didn't she file a report?"

"Nothing was taken. And then the other morning her things were disturbed in the gym locker, but again nothing was taken, so she didn't report that, either."

"How convenient."

Jason ignored the note of sarcasm. "All I know is that Albert was working at the gym that morning. He had the opportunity and the time. Now all you need to determine is his motive. At least interview him in an official capacity and ask why he's doing this, though I think I know why."

"You think? Yeah, that's the trouble with fiction writers. They think too much. First you think you can link a couple of murders that are ancient history in this town. Then you come back and try to twist your fiction into fact. Well, I don't need you to tell me how to do my job." Boyd flushed when he realized the head of the hotel security was watching and listening. He turned away abruptly. "I'll go see Albert right now and get to the bottom of this." As he started away he paused. "Just remember that all of this started when you returned to Devil's Cove. If you're doing this for publicity, I'll see you prosecuted to the limit."

When the valet held the door of his car Jason slid behind the wheel and paused to dial the number to Emily's clinic.

His tension eased when he heard Mel's voice on the machine. After the beep he said, "I see you've finished with your patients right on schedule, Dr. Brennan. Think you could spare me a few minutes of your time? I should be there soon. I'm leaving the Harbor House now."

His smile remained as he put the car in gear. If he hurried there was still time to set off a few fireworks of their own before the evening's festivities.

* * *

At the sound of Jason's voice on the message machine, Emily felt her heart soar. But one look at Albert's face had the panic returning. It was obvious that he wasn't about to be frightened off by Jason's arrival.

"I couldn't have planned this any better." He waved the knife and saw the way she stared at it with a sort of horrified fascination. He loved the sense of power this gave him. He stood a little taller. His voice rang with authority as he savored the moment. "Sit down on that stool in the corner."

When Emily didn't move quickly enough he gave her a shove, slamming her against the wall. "I said sit."

Dazed, she did as he ordered.

He gave a nod of approval. "Good. Now there's nothing to do but wait."

"For what?"

"For your lover boy to show up and the fun to begin."

"What fun, Albert?"

"Oh, I think you know, Doc."

Emily's throat was so dry, she could barely swallow. She thought of her grandparents, just a few rooms away. More than anything, she wanted them safe. Maybe, when Jason arrived, she could shout a warning, and he could at least see that they were taken to safety.

As if reading her mind Albert threw back his head and laughed. "I can see the wheels turning in that pretty little head, Doc. Sorry to spoil your plans."

He dragged her into his arms, holding the knife to her throat.

When Emily heard the crunch of footsteps outside the clinic door, her heart began pounding so wildly, she wondered that it didn't just rip clear through her chest.

"Emily?" Jason's voice was muffled through the closed door.

"She's in here." Albert yanked open the door to the examination room.

Jason paused on the threshold. The sight of Emily being held in Albert's arms, the blade of a knife to her throat, filled him with a blaze of white-hot fury.

"You don't want to hurt her, Albert."

"That's where you're wrong. I'm going to enjoy hurting her, just like I did those others. And this time, when I'm through with her, the whole town is going to call me a hero for catching the guy who killed all those poor innocent girls in the past."

Jason's eyes narrowed. "What are you talking about?"

"You may be a big rich writer now, but you're still the son of the town drunk. What are people going to think when there hasn't been a killing in Devil's Cove since you left town, and now, just a week after you're back, it's started again?" Albert gave a high, shrill laugh. "Add to that the message you left on the good doctor's machine, and the fact that your fingerprints are going to be all over this knife, and what we have here is exactly what you predicted in that book of yours. What did you call it? Oh yeah. *Secrets in a Small Town*. Well, after today, there won't be any more secrets. At long last, everyone will know the name of the infamous Devil's Cove serial killer."

Chapter 15

It tore at Jason's heart to see the fear in Emily's eyes. To see the blade of Albert's knife pressed to her throat. Whatever wild and confused feelings had slammed into him when he'd first caught sight of her being held at knifepoint, now there was only one. He was filled with an all-consuming need to keep her safe, no matter what the cost to himself.

For now, his best chance was to bide his time and keep this madman talking, rather than acting.

"You don't want to hurt Emily, Albert. She isn't like the others you killed."

The hand at her throat tightened perceptibly. "How would you know?"

"I researched the murders. I got to know the victims. I learned a lot about you, too."

"You never knew it was me. You were only guessing."

"That's right. I was. But it was an educated guess. I knew the murders were linked, even though there were years between them. I decided they were linked not only by the weapon of choice…" He flicked a glance at the knife, then back at Albert's face. "…but also by the killer's ability to get the girls to agree to be alone with him. What did you use, Albert? Physical force?"

A sly smile touched the old man's mouth. "Even better. A note from their teacher."

Emily's stomach gave a sickening lurch at the thought of a trusted teacher's name, perhaps even her own grandmother's, being used to lure three helpless girls to their deaths.

"As for the weapon, a gun makes too much noise. But a knife…" He caressed it with a quick slide of his finger. "…smooth as butter. And when it's handled by a pro, every bit as effective as a bullet."

"But why? Why did you have to kill those girls?" The question escaped Emily's lips before she could stop herself.

"Why?" Again that high, shrill laugh that

scraped over her nerves as his fingers dug into her shoulder. "Because they weren't nice. They needed to show a little respect. To them I was nothing more than a machine that fixed a leaky faucet or a plugged toilet. Did they think I didn't overhear their nasty little comments when they saw me on my hands and knees in the filth of the bathroom or furnace room? Did they think I had no feelings when they treated me like dirt?"

Jason needed to draw Albert's attention away from Emily. His hand was too tense. The knife's blade too close to her throat. "Is that what Cindy did?"

Albert blinked. "Was that her name? Huh." He gave a grunt of confusion. "Yeah. That's right. Cindy. Half undressed with some boy in the girl's bathroom when I walked in. She didn't even have the decency to act ashamed. She just laughed and said, 'You don't have to worry. It's only old Albert.'" His eyes narrowed. "Old Albert. I guess I showed her."

"What about the migrant worker who was found guilty in that crime?"

"He was so drunk I nearly stumbled over him. Lucky for me." He gave another laugh. "Unlucky for him."

"And the second girl? Mary Lou?"

"She caught me with some girlie pictures in the furnace room and threatened to turn me in to the school board. I had to work fast, so I slipped a note into her locker and signed the drama coach's name, asking her to stay after school and try out for a lead in the school play." He cackled at his own joke. "She got the lead, all right. I made her a star. She was in all the headlines the next day."

Jason gauged the distance between Albert and himself, wondering how many seconds it would take to yank Emily free. Enough to keep that knife from ripping through her flesh? He couldn't afford any wrong turns now. One misstep and he could be the cause of even more pain in the process.

"What did you do with the note?"

He gave a sly grin. "I made sure it disappeared."

"And Annette? The third girl?" Jason touched a hand to the examining table that stood between them. Too heavy to toss aside. Too high to leap over. He'd have to risk going around it, even though it would mean a few extra seconds.

"That little slut." Albert's grin faded. "She was older than the other two. Old enough to know what she was doing."

"What was she doing?" Jason very carefully planted his feet, slightly apart, and tensed.

"Teasing me. She'd stop by my office once a week on one pretense or another. One day she claimed she needed the master key to the lockers, because she'd lost hers. Another time she claimed a teacher had sent her to ask me to turn up the heat in the east wing of the school. She turned up my heat instead. I found out later that it was all a lie, to see how much I'd be willing to do for her. When I overheard her bragging to her friends that she'd found the perfect old fool to buy her booze for a beach party, I decided to have a little party of my own."

"So you got her drunk, and then drowned her instead of slitting her throat. Clever." Jason kept his voice soothing. "That explains not only why you wanted them hurt, but why the police couldn't link the murders. But why do you want to hurt Emily? She never showed you any disrespect, Albert."

"This isn't about the doc. It's about you."

"Then let her go and deal with me."

"You think I'm stupid? That's what they all thought. Stupid Albert. Dirty Albert. Drunk Albert." His lips peeled back in a feral snarl. "That's right. I know what they said about my drinking. Your dad was the only one who didn't think he was too good to drink with me."

"My father would have joined a nest of rattlers if they'd offered him a drink."

"You see?" Albert waved the knife about wildly. "You always thought you were better'n him. Better'n me, too. That day you lit out of town, I told your old man if you was my son I'd kill you."

"He tried to a number of times." Jason had to fight to keep his tone even. Even now, after all these years, he could barely speak of his father without feeling the pain.

"And still you came back. This is your fault. If you hadn't written your stupid book, no one would have given those dead girls a thought. It would have all gone along like before, and the doc could have lived. But now she'll have to pay the price."

"For sleeping with me?"

"For mattering to you."

"Is that why you've been stalking us?"

"I had to learn your weakness. Everybody has one. Let's see how big and smart and important you are when I take away the thing that matters most to you." The sly look was back. "I bet you thought I didn't even know about your book, or the fact that it was about me."

"I was describing a fictional killer. One I saw only in my own mind."

''Then how come you made him look like me? Sound like me? Drink like me?''

''The similarity was only in your mind. In fact, I really ought to thank you, Albert, for exorcising my worst demon. You see, all along, while researching the book, while writing it, I thought the one who'd killed those girls was my father.''

''Liar. You knew it was me.'' Albert's eyes narrowed. ''When you showed up for Mrs. B.'s tribute, I figured it was a sign. The old Albert, Evil Albert, needed to come back one more time.''

''Is that what you called yourself while you were killing those girls?''

''That's right.'' He gave a sly wink. ''It was Evil Albert. He was the one killed them. He's the one holding the knife to the doc's throat right now.''

''All right, Evil Albert. Why the break-ins?''

''To watch you sweat.'' Albert gave a short laugh. ''That night I was here in the clinic, I could see all this in my mind. Where I would stand. How you'd look when you realized I was going to kill the woman you loved. And how you'd beg for mercy when I started cutting her.'' He pressed the blade of the knife against Emily's throat.

Jason knew the time for talk was over. Unless he moved now, Emily would pay the price.

He hurled himself against Albert, slamming him

against the wall, while at the same instant wrenching Emily from his grasp and flinging her aside with such force she fell to her knees.

"Run, Em," he shouted as he closed both hands around Albert's wrist, struggling to wrestle the knife from his grasp.

"She's not going anywhere, and neither are you." Albert butted his head into Jason's midsection, driving him to the floor. In the blink of an eye he straddled him, and lifted the knife high, taking aim at Jason's heart.

Seeing that Emily had flung open the drug cabinet, Albert shouted, "If you try anything stupid, Doc, I'll kill him."

When she hesitated Jason said, "He's going to kill me anyway. Save yourself, Emily."

But it wasn't her own life she was concerned with now.

Before Albert could drive his weapon home Jason swung his arm in an arc, feeling the blade bite deep into his hand before clattering to the floor. Ignoring the blood that spurted from Jason's wound, the two men rolled around and around the floor, scrambling for possession of the knife.

Just as Jason managed to close a hand around the handle, he felt a blow to his head that had him seeing stars. By the time his vision cleared, Albert was once again straddling him. This time the sharp edge of the knife was against his throat.

"It would've been more fun for me if you could've been around to watch the doc die, but I can't wait any longer to have my revenge." Albert leaned forward to finish the deed.

Suddenly he stiffened, and his eyes went vacant. As he slumped forward, Jason scrambled aside and watched as the knife slipped from his nerveless fingers.

He looked up to see Emily holding a syringe. Though her face had lost all its color, and her legs were trembling, she managed to cry, "Oh, Jason, I thought I was going to be too late to save you."

"You were just in time." Because he was too exhausted to stand, he caught her hand and drew her down to his arms.

They looked up when Boyd Thompson came rushing into the room, followed by several of his officers. "I've been looking everywhere for..." He stopped short and stared at the bloody mess that littered the floor, and the still figure of Albert Sneed. "Is he dead?"

Emily shook her head. "Out cold. I injected him with a full shot of Dilaudin. It'll take several hours before he'll be alert enough to answer any of your questions."

Boyd knelt and touched a finger to Albert's neck, before turning to Emily and Jason. "I'm really sorry. I got it into my head that your book was an indictment of my father's work, and I let that color my judgment. By the time I realized that you might have a valid complaint against Albert, I'd wasted a lot of precious time." While his officers began to photograph the scene, he helped Jason and Emily to their feet and led them to the outer office.

They slumped down on the sofa in the waiting room, clinging together.

Boyd stood facing them. "You have every right to file a formal complaint against me for my behavior."

Jason kept one arm around Emily, to assure himself that she was really safe. "I don't want you to lose your badge or your job, Boyd."

"You don't? Do you realize that if you file a complaint, the county's review board would launch a full-scale investigation?"

Jason managed a grim smile. "I'm not interested in county investigations or review boards. From now on I'll happily settle for fictional criminals who live only in my head."

Emily breathed a quiet sigh of relief before taking his hand in hers. "This will need stitches."

He shot her a grin. "Know a good doctor?"

For the first time in what seemed an eternity, she found her smile. "As a matter of fact, I do."

"Better make it quick." He wondered why everything looked so normal. The office. The police chief. The woman who was holding his hand. Maybe it would all come crashing down on him later. But for now, for this moment, the woman he loved was safe, and the madman who had spent a lifetime hiding his crimes was now effectively out of commission. "We have a banquet to attend."

"Don't forget the fireworks." Boyd cleared his throat, wondering if either of them was even aware that he was still there. From the looks of them, they'd gone off somewhere to their own little world.

"Oh, you can count on that. There's definitely going to be fireworks."

At Jason's words Emily looked at him and felt her heart do a strange little somersault. Then she laughed, a clear, lilting sound, as giddy relief washed over her.

When Boyd and his officers took their leave, bearing Albert on a gurney, Jason and Emily were still standing, arms locked around each other, foreheads pressed together, laughing like two children, mumbling incoherent words about fireworks.

Epilogue

"**Y**ou're late." Hannah speared a strawberry that garnished her fruit tart and watched as Emily and Jason took their places at the table reserved for Bert and her family. "I hope it was worth missing the best fried chicken on earth."

Emily couldn't stop the smile from lighting her eyes. "It was."

The school auditorium was packed with people enjoying the banquet catered by the chefs from the Harbor House.

The judge pointed to Jason's hand. "A little accident?"

Jason grinned and lowered his hand to his lap. "Yeah."

"That's what comes of being a writer. Soft hands. Doing a bit of research, no doubt."

"You might say that." Jason and Emily shared a smile.

Sidney leaned close to whisper, "Good thing you didn't miss the fireworks, too."

"Yeah." Jason winked at Emily, who seemed unusually flushed. "They're the best part."

The principal of the school mounted the steps and paused before the microphone on stage.

"It's been quite a day." His words echoed across the room as he stared knowingly at Emily and Jason. After much wrangling, the authorities had agreed to keep the news of Albert Sneed a secret until Bert's tribute ended. The morning edition of the local newspaper would carry the story, and it would no doubt be picked up by the national media, with all its attending frenzy. But for now, this last night belonged to Mrs. B.

The principal lifted a glass of champagne. "Would you join me in a toast to our town's most beloved teacher."

The room was filled with the sound of chairs being scraped back and shuffling feet as everyone stood and turned toward Bert, seated at the head table.

"To Alberta Brennan, for a lifetime of service to the most important members of our community—our children."

The crowd erupted into thunderous applause.

The principal held up his hand until the crowd fell silent. "And now, after that delicious feast, we invite you to make yourselves comfortable out on the lawn of Harbor House. The barge is just offshore, and the fireworks display is about to begin."

As Jason and Emily set out with her family, Courtney nudged them. "Did you see Prentice and Will Osborn?"

Emily craned her neck. "Where?"

"Up ahead. They were having dinner with Carrie and her daughter, Jenny."

Emily sighed. "He finally found the courage to ask her."

"Ask her what?"

"For a date." Emily chuckled. "It's only taken him ten years."

"Better late than never." As the others surged past, Jason caught her hand and held her back.

"We'll lose our place." Emily glanced at the others who continued walking across the sloping lawn toward the waterfront.

"No, we won't. In fact, I think we've both just found it."

She arched a brow. "What's that supposed to mean?"

He glanced down at their joined hands. "Tell me something, Em. Are you still considering going back to University Hospital?"

She gave a negligent shrug of her shoulders. "It's becoming less and less appealing as the weeks go by. I think I like being back here." She swallowed. "What about you, Jason? Are you eager to get back to Malibu?"

"It lost its appeal the minute I saw you." At her quick smile he said, "There's something I have to tell you. I started to earlier, but was interrupted before I could finish. You asked why I never contacted you."

She wasn't even aware of the fact that she was holding her breath.

"The reason I was able to leave Devil's Cove the day after graduation is because a very generous person gave me enough money for a one-way ticket out of town."

"Who…?"

He held up a hand. "But there were strings attached to his gift. I wasn't to contact his daughter, or try to influence her life in any way, until she had made her own way in the world.''

"His...daughter?" As the truth dawned, she took a step back as though she'd been struck. "My father? But why? Why would he be so...coldly manipulative?"

"That's your term. He'd probably call it being a concerned father. Think about it, Emily. What was he supposed to do about a brilliant but head-strong daughter who was wildly in love with a loser with no future? He was desperate. And though what he did may have been manipulative, it gave us both the time we needed to grow up."

"And grow apart."

"For a while." He touched a hand to her shoulder. "I went to your grandmother for advice. She disapproved of the conditions, but she told me to take what he offered, since it was my only chance to break away from a life that was bound to take me down. She said, also, that if you and I were meant to be together, it would happen in time."

"In time." Emily lifted a hand to his cheek. "How did you survive all alone?"

"I found, to my amazement, just how strong and resilient I could be." He shook his head, remembering. "I've never been so lonely. Especially for you. But I made it, and I grew stronger and smarter along the way. And now, in retrospect, I realize that your father was right. If I had stayed, I would have taken you down. That wasn't what I wanted for you, Emily.''

''What did you want?''

''The same thing I want now. You. This.'' He nodded toward the crowd settling down on blankets and quilts on the sloping lawn of the Harbor House. ''If you'll have it, I'd like to share my life with you, Em.''

In the gathering darkness they heard the boom and saw the first brilliant flash of light as the fireworks display began.

''I've been waiting such a long time to hear you say that. But it was worth the wait.'' Emily wrapped her arms around his neck. Against his lips she whispered, ''Welcome home, Jason Cooper.''

''I like the sound of that. Home.'' As another brilliant display lit up the sky, and the crowd cheered, Jason drew her close and covered her mouth in a kiss that seemed to spin on and on, leaving them both breathless.

He knew now that it wasn't just this place, or the familiar people he'd known for a lifetime. It was this woman. In her arms he had truly come home.

*   *   *   *   *

*Curious about the other members of the amazing
Brennan family?
Meet Hannah in* Wanted,
*book two in Ruth Langan's
brand new series,*
DEVIL'S COVE.
*Available in April 2005 from
Silhouette Sensation.*

Turn the page for a sneak preview…

Wanted

by

Ruth Langan

Ethan Harrison awoke to the sound of a foghorn, and for a moment he thought he was back in Maine. He actually reached across the bed for Elizabeth before the realization struck. This wasn't Maine. He was in his new home in Michigan. And Elizabeth would never share his bed again.

He slipped into a pair of faded shorts and a T-shirt before padding down the hallway to the big room his two young sons shared. Seeing that they were both still asleep, he made his way down the stairs to the kitchen and plugged in the coffee maker before rummaging through the cupboards for cereal.

He carried the bowl and spoon out to the big wooden deck that looked out over Lake Michigan, and settled down on the top step with his back against the rail. Fog and mist rolled over him in damp waves, leaving his skin chilled.

The morning was as bleak as his mood. He'd come to Michigan to get as far away from the past as possible. But now he realized that the real lure of this place had been its proximity to water. If he had to leave everything that was comfortable and familiar, at least he would have some of it in his new surroundings. Of course, the fact that Devil's Cove was small and secluded was an important factor as well. He wanted, needed desperately, to find a safe haven for his sons.

He'd known the minute he saw this place, that it was exactly what he'd been hoping for. Though his yard ran right down to the water's edge, a sand-bar just offshore formed a natural barrier, making it impossible for a boat to get close enough to come ashore. The fact that this was a private, gated community, restricting all but those whose names were posted with a guard, made it all the better. He'd permitted his real estate agent to post the names of workers who required access to it. All others would require his express approval before being allowed on the premises.

The sweeping grounds, with more than an acre

of aged trees hiding a tall iron fence, made it appear to be just another millionaire's retreat, though Ethan considered it more a fortress.

A fortress. The thought added to his gloom. He hated having to lock his sons away from the world, but for now, it seemed the only solution.

At the sound of tires crunching on the gravel drive he looked up to see a truck roll to a stop. Seconds later the truck's door opened and a figure in torn jeans walked to the tailgate and began tugging on a heavy tarp.

Curious, Ethan set aside his empty bowl and strolled over. "Need a hand?"

"Thanks."

At the decidedly feminine voice, he found himself stepping back to stare.

"You work for the contractor?" She kept her back to him as she began retrieving shovels and rakes and tossing them to him.

"Afraid not." He couldn't help admiring the long, long legs and trim backside as he set each tool aside in the grass.

"Oh." She glanced over her shoulder and he had a quick impression of pale blond hair beneath the baseball cap, and eyes the color of honey, before she turned back to her work. "Did Martin hire you?"

"Martin?"

"My crew boss." She retrieved the last of the equipment and brushed her hands down her pants before turning to him. Her smile was absolutely captivating. "Are you a new hire?"

"Sorry. No."

She looked him up and down, considering. "Then what are you doing here at this time of the morning?"

"I live here."

"You live…?" She stopped and her smile turned impish. "Oops. You must be the new owner. I thought you weren't moving in until next week."

"I decided to get an early start. And you'd be…?"

"Hannah Brennan." She stuck out her hand. "Hannah's Gardening and Landscape. I was hired to do your yard."

"Ah. Ethan Harrison." He latched onto the only thing that his brain could manage in the presence of that dazzling smile and firm handshake. "Brennan. Are you related to Charlotte, my real estate agent?"

"My mother. But nobody calls her Charlotte. Around here, she's Charley."

"Charley. I'll remember that." His smile widened. "She came highly recommended by an old college friend. I don't know what I'd have done without her.''

Hannah nodded. "She's the best."

"I'll say. After only a few questions over the phone, she seemed to know exactly what I had in mind. It only took her a few days to get back to me with a list of several places she wanted me to see. When I flew out here, I expected to spend weeks making a decision. But the minute I saw this place, I knew it was the one."

Hannah looked beyond him to study the house, one of several million-dollar mansions that had recently been built on waterfront acreage that had been part of an old orchard. "It's a great place. And this view…" She didn't bother to finish the sentence, allowing the sight of sunlight breaking through the mist over the water to speak for itself.

Ethan nodded. "It was the view that sold me." He didn't bother to mention the security.

He glanced back at the truck. "So you're going to turn this weed patch into a lawn and gardens, are you?"

"That's what I do best." She smiled. "I don't have to get started today, though. I didn't realize you'd moved in. You probably have a million things to see to. If you'd like me to schedule another time…"

"No. You certainly won't be in my way. I think

it'll be fun to watch the lawn and gardens take shape and…''

At the peals of laughter Hannah turned toward the deck in time to see two little boys dressed in pajamas barreling down the steps and launching themselves into their father's arms.

Ethan caught the two in a bear hug and swung them around before setting them on their bare feet in the grass. "TJ. Danny. This is Hannah Brennan."

Hannah knelt down and offered her handshake. The older of the two stuck out his hand.

"Are you TJ or Danny?"

"Danny."

"Hi, Danny. How old are you?"

"I'm four." He held up four fingers.

"So old? And what about your little brother?"

He grinned and pointed to the toddler holding tightly to his father's ankle. "TJ's two."

"Two," the little boy echoed.

"What does TJ stand for?"

"Thaddeus Joseph," Danny said proudly, causing his little brother to grin widely.

"That's quite a mouthful for such a little guy. No wonder you call him TJ."

"Uh-huh. Daddy says I'm a big boy."

"It's nice to be a big brother."

"Do you have one?"

Hannah shook her head. "Just sisters. I have a big sister and two little sisters."

"Do you have to watch out for them when they're playing?"

"I did when they were younger. Now they're big enough to look out for themselves."

He eyed her truck. "Is that yours?"

"Yeah." She got to her feet. "Do you like it?"

He nodded. "It's bigger'n Daddy's car."

"Is it?" She glanced over at Ethan and winked. "Well, he only has to haul two little boys around, but I have to haul a crew of workers, as well as a lot of tools."

"Wow." The little boys eyed her with respect. "You work with tools?"

"Shovels. Rakes. Trenchers. Tractors."

"Tractors?" Danny turned to his father with a shriek of delight. "Can I watch the tractors?"

Ethan got down on one knee. "You can. As long as you and TJ stay on the deck, where you'll be safe. Tractors can be fun to watch, but they can be deadly if the driver can't see you." He glanced over his son's head. "Danny has been in love with trucks and tractors since he was a baby. In fact, he has an entire construction yard ready to be set up in his bedroom. If we can find which box it's in."

Hannah looked impressed. "I'd like to see that sometime, Danny."

"Can I show her, Daddy?"

Ethan nodded. "I don't see why not. Another time. Right now, I think we'd better get inside and I'll fix the two of you some breakfast."

His little son turned to look at Hannah. "Are you going to drive a tractor here today?"

"Not for a couple of days." She slipped off her baseball cap and ran a hand through her hair. "Today I'm just going to do a walk-around and decide where everything will go. Then, after your daddy approves my design sketches, I'll get my crew started."

"One day will you come inside and see my trucks?"

"I'd like that." She grinned at the younger boy, who clung to his father's leg.

As the two little boys scampered toward the house, Ethan turned back. "I think I'd better warn you. Now that Danny has found someone who drives a truck and a tractor, he may become something of a pest. Whenever he gets in the way, just let me know."

Hannah gave a shake of her head, sending blond wisps dancing. "I wouldn't worry about it. It's sort of flattering to find a guy who isn't put off by the fact that I drive a truck."

She turned away and busied herself folding the tarp. Minutes later she heard the door slam, and

the peals of laughter from the kitchen told her that
father and sons were enjoying their breakfast.

While Hannah and her crew chief completed
their inspection of the yard, Hannah made crude
sketches on a clipboard.

"Ground cover in that shady area." She pointed
with her pencil. "And I'm thinking maybe a per-
ennial garden over there."

Martin Cross nodded his agreement. "What
about those old forsythia and lilac?"

Hannah shrugged. "I don't want to tear out anything more than necessary. Part of the charm of
this property is the mature plants, left from its former life. But if they prove to be more dead wood
than blooms, we'll have to yank them."

"I'll take some cuttings and see what I find."

"Thanks, Martin." Hannah paused beneath an
ancient oak. The gnarled, twisted limbs lent a dig-
nified beauty to the yard, despite the fact that the
ground beneath was too densely shaded to allow
any grass to grow.

BOOK Offer Exclusive to Silhouette Romance Series

Buy this book and get another free! Simply indicate which series you are interested in by ticking the box and we'll send you a FREE book.
Please tick only one box

✂

Special Edition	❏	Superromance	❏
Sensation	❏	Intrigue	❏
Desire	❏	Spotlight	❏

Please complete the following:

Name _____

Address _____

_____ Postcode _____

Please cut out and return the above coupon along with your till receipt to:

**Silhouette Free Book competition,
Reader Service
FREEPOST NAT 10298, Richmond,
Surrey TW9 1BR**

▼ SILHOUETTE®
Sensation™

IN THE DARK
by international bestselling author
Heather Graham

Alexandra McCord's life was unravelling.
The body she'd discovered had
disappeared—and now she was trapped on
an island with a hurricane roaring in and
threatening her life. The only man she
could rely on was David Denham, the ex-
husband she'd never forgotten. But was he
her saviour—or a killer?

'This book is impossible to put down…'
—*Romantic Times*

ALSO AVAILABLE NEXT MONTH

WANTED by Ruth Langan
Devil's Cove

AGAINST THE WALL by Lyn Stone
Special Ops

SHOCK WAVES by Jenna Mills

ONE EYE OPEN by Karen Whiddon
Shivers

BULLETPROOF BRIDE by Diana Duncan

On sale 18th March 2005

Visit our website at www.silhouette.co.uk

Available at most branches of WHSmith, Tesco, ASDA, Martins,
Borders, Eason, Sainsbury's and most good paperback bookshops.

SILHOUETTE®
Sensation™

proudly presents an exhilarating new series

Shivers

Adventure, excitement and
supernatural love...

*Perfect for fans of Buffy, Anne Rice, Kelly
Armstrong and The Pirates of the Caribbean*

DARKNESS CALLS by Caridad Piñeiro
January 2005
A vampire helps an FBI agent find a psychotic killer,
and promises her eternal love.

ONE EYE OPEN by Karen Whiddon
April 2005
Can love blossom between a scarred man and
a female werewolf?

GHOST OF A CHANCE by Nina Bruhns
July 2005
A writer gets more than she bargains for when she
meets the man of her dreams—a sexy pirate ghost
under a 200 year old curse!

0205/SH/LC103

SILHOUETTE®
Sensation™

*is proud to present
an exciting new series from popular author*

LYN STONE

SPECIAL OPS

DANGEROUS. DEADLY. DESIRABLE.

Six top agents with unparalleled skills are
united to create an unbeatable team.

Their mission: eliminate terrorist threats
to the US – at home and abroad.

DOWN TO THE WIRE
February 2005

AGAINST THE WALL
April 2005

UNDER THE GUN
June 2005

Visit our website at www.silhouette.co.uk

FREE!

4 Books
and a surprise gift!

We would like to take this opportunity to thank you for reading this Silhouette® book by offering you the chance to take FOUR more specially selected titles from the Sensation™ series absolutely FREE! We're also making this offer to introduce you to the benefits of the Reader Service™—

- ★ **FREE home delivery**
- ★ **FREE gifts and competitions**
- ★ **FREE monthly Newsletter**
- ★ **Exclusive Reader Service offers**
- ★ **Books available before they're in the shops**

Accepting these FREE books and gift places you under no obligation to buy, you may cancel at any time, even after receiving your free shipment. Simply complete your details below and return the entire page to the address below. You don't even need a stamp!

YES! Please send me 4 free Sensation books and a surprise gift. I understand that unless you hear from me, I will receive 6 superb new titles every month for just £3.05 each, postage and packing free. I am under no obligation to purchase any books and may cancel my subscription at any time. The free books and gift will be mine to keep in any case.

S5ZEF

Ms/Mrs/Miss/Mr ....Initials ....
BLOCK CAPITALS PLEASE

Surname ....

Address ....

....

....Postcode ....

Send this whole page to:
UK: FREEPOST CN81, Croydon, CR9 3WZ